Sex, Secrets and Scandal

A NOVEL

Deborah Caren Langley

G000068360

Temptation Sealed

Temptation Sealed

This edition published by Inscape Solutions Limited

Copyright © 2022 by Deborah Caren Langley

Deborah Caren Langley asserts the moral right to be identified as the author of this work.

A catalogue record for this work is available from The British Library

ISBN:	Softcover	
	eBook	978-1-3999-1948-7

I am Deborah Caren Langley. I write because I love creating storylines and creating characters. I love to watch my characters come alive and take on a personality all of their own. I hope that when you read my books you see and feel it too.

Apart from my family, nothing has given me so much joy as writing so I've kept going. This is my fifth book – I hope you enjoy reading it as much as I did writing it.

Acknowledgements

I would like thank my publisher, Nigel Wilkins, to whom I owe a debt of gratitude.

Also, I would like to thank every wonderful, romantic person out there for buying and reading my books. Also, for the wonderful reviews you have all given me, they are truly appreciated.

So thank so much. You keep reading and I'll keep writing…

Prologue

A sister's' love is a bond that should never be broken, a love that is unconditional and built on trust. Sisters look out for each other, protect and care for each other. Zella and Patsy Russell were no different. They told each other everything and had no secrets but that was about to change.

When the truth finally comes out, what will Zella and Patsy do? Is that very special bond to be destroyed or can the damage be repaired?

Read on and see what happens to these sisters. Just how strong is their bond?

Chapter 1

April 1955

Patsy ran in through the back door and into the kitchen like a bat out of hell, puffing, panting and spluttering like wild animal. She ran in so fast that she cannoned straight into the table, knocking the crockery flying. Just in the nick of time Zella caught the cup that was wobbling its way to the edge.

"Patsy, what on earth? …Calm down!"

Patsy was so excited she couldn't get her words out, she didn't even take a breath between sentences.

"I have just met the most handsome man…"

Before she could finish their mum, Florence, entered the kitchen. She'd heard all the commotion and wanted to know what all the excitement was about.

Patsy went on to tell them she was in love.

"He has jet black hair and biggest grey eyes you've ever seen."

"Who has?" Asked Zella.

"I don't know his name, but I'm going to marry him…"

"What man?" Their mother chipped in sternly.

"I met him today."

"I want to know who this man is, Patsy."

"What on earth has happened to George?" Zella asked, sounding a little confused.

"George is gone, I don't love him… I love the man I met today."

Patsy started to tell them about the handsome young man she had met in the cafe that day. Florence, however, wasn't happy. Patsy had been going steady with George since she left school and everyone assumed they would eventually marry. She did not like idea of her daughter flirting with men she hardly knew and she demanded to know all about this young man who had made her daughter so giddy.

Pasty explained that she had only just met him and she would bring him round when she had got to know him a little better, Florence was adamant she wanted to meet him if he was going to be courting her daughter. After all, this sort of thing didn't happen in her day. When she met Willard you simply got wed and settled down to married life.

Willard worked a thirteen hour day in the cotton mill as a vertical opener and scutcher while Florence would stay at home and looked after the home front and care for their children. There was none of this dreamy-eyed nonsense.

Florence was a strong minded woman. She had to be, she had been left on her own with two young daughters when Willard had died in the war. It had been long and hard during the war what with the blackouts because of the night bombings by the Luftwaffe, raids drills and sirens.

They would hear the air raid warning 'attack in progress', then the all clear siren. It was very frightening for anyone, let alone small children.

It was especially hard for Florence when, like so many others, she received that dreadful telegram telling her that among the husbands, sons and fathers shot and killed in the line of duty was her Willard. Nearly 2,000 people were killed or wounded in London's first night of the blitz. But that was then.

Zella was her eldest, nineteen now with mousey brown, shoulder length bouffant-styled hair whereas Patsy was seventeen, also with mousy brown hair but cut shorter in an Italian style. They both had blue eyes and were about medium height. They were very close, nobody ever came between them. They defended each other no matter what, their love for each other was unconditional.

January 1955 – Where it all began

Patsy worked in the café in the town centre. She knew all the customers and everyone thought her pleasant and well-mannered. Zella loved fashion and the latest trends and worked at the local boutique. They were promoting a new line in the store and a local journalist, Alden Pearce, was coming in to write the story for the *News Echo*, Stan Lindon's local rag. Zella loved to make her own clothes and, even more, thinking up new designs. She wasn't without talent either and had lots of designs tucked away. She dreamt of some day having her own label and owning her own shop. Her dreams were pretty big, sometimes she thought they were too big, but nonetheless they were *her* dreams.

Alden and his friend Derick had also lost their families in the war. Early on, they had been among the many the evacuees in Operation *Pied Piper*, escaping the city centre bombs in the countryside. Their fathers had been killed in action while Alden had lost his mother and sister in the Blitz in London. He had been wandering around in a daze when a war reserve police officer spotted him and took him to the church hall where there were many more children, including Derick. He had been taken there after he was separated from his mother. He found out later she had been killed in a blast, along with his unborn sibling.

The boys were among the more than 3.5million evacuated to the countryside, to places such Wales or Devon, even overseas. They ended up in rural Wales, placed with the same family. They grow up together and became more like brothers than friends. They looked out for each other, after all, they only had each other. Together they worked on the farm with their family hosts until the war was over. When peace was announced, it was a time to rejoice. The church bells rang and there were parties and celebrations everywhere.

When the time came for Alden and Derick to leave the countryside and the family hosts behind, they were just sixteen and had no-one other than themselves to rely on. They would travel from place to place looking for work and they worked hard, never taking anything unless it was work for the two of them. They had lived in Huddersfield for two years then Bradford for two more. It didn't matter what they went for, Alden somehow always seemed to be able to talk them both in to a job.

They had just arrived in Chesterfield when Alden saw that the local newspaper was recruiting journalists and, without them having any experience whatsoever, somehow he talked them both in to the job. According to him, Alden was a good talker and Derrick was a great photographer .

As it happened, they took to it like ducks to water and that won Stan over. Mind you, they had to work hard to prove themselves.

One of Alden's first assignments was to interview Peggy at the Boutique *Special Something*. When Peggy introduced Zella, Alden's jaw dropped. All he could do was stand there with his mouth open staring at her, he couldn't take his eyes from her. He just had to ask her out on a date but he didn't have the nerve.

After that, he went in every day for a week, wandering round the boutique looking nervously in the men's section. Every now and then he would look up at Zella and run it through his head how to ask her to go out with him but every time he got close, his nerves got the better of him. He didn't normally have this problem but he simply got tongue tied every time he saw her, she just took his breath away.

She would smile at him every time he came in the store because Peggy had mentioned the fact he liked her.

"No… he's so handsome… I'm not his type."

"Zella, Darling… Why do you think he comes here every day?"

"Maybe he likes the clothes?"

"And how many do you think is interested in?"

"OK… Maybe to see how the article is doing?"

Peggy shook her head and giggled, "And when does he ask about the article?"

Zella blushed.

"Don't look now but... I think he's checking how far your seams go up on your stockings."

"Ohhhh... No he isn't... Is he?"

"Uhhhh... yes I think he is."

"Oh... My goodness," then she gave a cheeky giggle.

When they looked over at Alden, he looked quite nervous and quickly left the shop. When he met up with Derick, Derick asked where he'd been. Alden quickly made some excuse up.

"You wouldn't be lying would you, my old buddy?"

"Why would I lie to you?"

"Because pal you have been acting very shifty this past week"

"Shifty...?"

"Yep..."

"Alright... I have met someone."

"Ha! Ha! That explains it."

The following week Alden looked in through the shop window to see if he could see Zella then took a deep breath and thought, *'here goes'*. As he walked straight up to her he could feel his nerves kicking in, but the little voice in his head was telling him to ask her out. "Go on, go on," it said.

"Hey..." He smiled. "I was wondering..."

"Wondering.... What?"

"Please don't stop me – I'll lose my nerve..."

Zella smiles but stayed silent, biting her bottom lip with excitement

"…Would you like to go out with me?" He didn't even stop to breathe.

Zella laughed at the speed it all came out of his mouth and she promptly accepted.

"Oh…Ohhhh… fantastic"

Then he asked where she lived. Zella told him that she would meet him at the old picture house as she didn't want her mother to know anything about her meeting Alden, otherwise she would have got twenty questions, she knew her mother so well. She didn't even tell Patsy.

That evening they met at the picture house to see *'Without the Rain'* a romantic comedy which wasn't really Alden's thing, but Zella had told him how much she wanted to see it. The film was a low budget film directed by a new director called Matt Adams, but Zella enjoyed it. Alden watched her every reaction to the romantic scenes. When the couples in the film kissed, her eyes glazed over in dreamy haze. He thought she was simply beautiful and he loved the fact she got so excited at the smallest detail.

Alden didn't want her to disappear straight after the film so he suggested they got some chips and Zella thought that was a lovely idea. So, soon they were walking slowly along the canal bank eating their chips, there was something just so good about eating your chips from a newspaper. They talked about their dreams and ambitions and seemed to have so much in common. They were both very ambitious – he wanted to be a big news reporter and Zella wanted to be a big name designer.

"Do you like being a reporter?"

"Yes... I want to work for a big name newspaper someday."

"I would like to have my own label on clothes one day."

"Let hope we both achieve our dreams," as he held out a chip. "We haven't any drink so let's clink chips." He chuckled.

Zella laughed and held out her chip. Solemnly, he bumped her chip and they both laughed. He was the perfect gentleman after that, he made sure she got the bus home safely as she would only let him to take to the bus stop.

By now, they had been seeing each other for months, meeting two or three times a week at the old picture house or the coffee shop near where she worked. Alden had never been with anyone long enough to be presented to the parents but he had fallen for Zella and fallen hard. So, he wanted to meet her mum, he thought it was time to be introduced but Zella wanted to wait just a little longer. When he asked why she informed him that her mother was very strict and would grill him with questions upon questions. He said he didn't mind.

"I just want to keep it like this for a little longer."

"Alright... but soon."

Zella didn't want that yet, she liked the fact that it was just the two of them and wanted to keep it that way for a bit longer. She'd had fallen in love with Alden. He had been the only one she was willing to give herself to.

One Saturday they headed off to Renishaw Hall and Gardens. It was a beautiful big old house that had been there for 400 hundred years ,possibly more. They took a long walk to the ballroom gardens then through the woodland. Running along the woodland was the lakeside, along with a colourful boarder of flowers,

Alden put his jacket down for Zella to sit on whilst he took his sandwiches, well door stops to be precise, from the satchel together with a couple of fruit buns and two bottles of elderflower pop. Zella fought her way through her sandwich whilst soaking up the unique atmosphere

"This is beautiful…" She sighed.

"I like it here."

"Have you brought a lot of girls here?"

"Why did you ask that? I have never brought any girls here."

"Uhhhh, I'm sorry Alden… I didn't mean anything by it."

"You are the only girl I have brought here."

Before she could say another word, he leant over to kiss her. She suddenly got lost in his passionate kiss. She knew he was the only man she would ever love, she knew she was ready to take that next step. Breaking from her trance, they strolled back hand in hand, smiling at each other.

He asked if he could see her the next day. Unfortunately Zella had to decline as her mother always made a Sunday dinner and she expected Zella and Patsy at the table. He told her he understood and they arranged to meet up on the following Tuesday evening to go to the cinema. Monday was the night both of them had plans with their friends.

Zella had gone out with her friend Dotty and Alden had gone to meet Derick. They were both quiet and they were both thinking about the other.

Alden and Derick had gone to a co-workers house for a friendly game of cards. They would only bet a penny a game and every time Alden won he would put that extra penny away. He wasn't bad at cards either so he won a good few pennies. Derick asked what he was going to do with the pennies he'd won.

"I'm saving up for something."

"Oh I see…"

It couldn't have been for a car as he had a car – an old banger, maybe, but still a car.

"What are you saving for? I know, a nicer car."

"If you like."

That did not answer Derick's question. What wasn't Alden telling him? He usually told him everything unless the money was something for him. Yes, that had to be it, but he didn't need any money and his birthday wasn't for a while yet so no, that couldn't be it. Derick was at a loss, what did Alden need the extra money for? He had a whole scenario going round his head then it dawned on him, Alden had got a girl in the family way! There again, Alden would surely have told him about that, He would just have to wait and see.

Meanwhile at Dotty house, Dotty asked Zella what was wrong with her as she was behaving very oddly. Zella simply replied.

"Nothing… everything is wonderful."

"Have you met someone Zella?"

Zella just smiled.

"You have!" Dotty interrupted her.

"Maybe…"

"Have you done it?"

"Done what?"

"You know what I mean, Zella Russell"

"If you are referring to *S.E.X.*, then No, I haven't."

"Ohhhh damn it… I want to know what it's like."

"Well, I don't know."

"Don't you wonder what it's like to have a man wrap his strong arms around you and take you, make love to you?"

"Dotty…"She giggled. "Actually Yes, I do wonder what that would be like."

Zella suggested that they need to get off this subject in case Dotty's parents heard them and thought it would be a good idea if they put the radio on. Dotty put the new singing sensation Alvin Preston on.

"Have you heard this one yet Zella?"

"What is it?"

"It's Alvin Preston's song, *My eyes Follow*"

They lay back on the bed and dreamily listen to the sexy tones of Alvin Preston's voice.

The following day after work she ran for the trolley bus so she could get back home to get ready to meet Alden. Patsy was already getting ready to meet George.

"You look lovely, Patsy"

"Thanks…"

"I thought you and George had broken up."

"Well sort of … I like George but that spark isn't there, you know?"

"Spark…?"

"Yeah ya know… the knee trembling, heart racing thing."

"Patsy… don't let mum hear you say this stuff."

"Come on Zella, you know that feeling… surely you must have felt it?"

"Well… No. I haven't ever had a serious boyfriend A couple of dates, Yes…"

She wasn't about to tell Patsy about Alden, she might blab to their mother. They told each other everything and this was the first time Zella had kept anything from her, but Patsy couldn't keep a secret for more than two seconds. Zella didn't want her mum to know just yet. Patsy laughed and planted a big kiss on Zella's cheek.

"Gotta go. See ya later, Zell!"

"Yeah… see ya later."

When Zella was ready she gave her mum a kiss and ran for the trolley bus to meet Alden. Alden was waiting in his car, he'd even cleaned it up. They went to the cinema to see *Borderline Rebel*, a rock 'n' roll musical. Some time later they drove to Lover's Cove, down near the canal bank where all the young couples went.

The moon was shining softly down on the car as they sat looking into each other's eyes as if they were looking in to each other's souls. He whispered softly that he loved her and leant in to kiss her. She had no wish for it to end, a girl could lose herself in his kiss. His thumb caressed her cheek as he kissed her, creating a burning sensation that was spreading through her body, swirling with emotion. He began to move his hands up to her breasts, undoing her button on her dress

"I want to make love to you, Zella, but I don't want you to think I'm trying to rush you."

"I want you to make love to me."

He looked at her closely, asking her if she was sure she wanted to do this. She smiled at him softly and simply replied, "Yes."

He gently pushed her dress up, removing her panties, all the while looking straight into her eyes. He pulled his manhood from his trousers slowly, moving himself her between thighs and pushing himself gently into her. He was so gentle and patient, then she gave a gasp.

"Am I hurting you?" He asked.

"It's alright."

"Are you sure?"

He moved slowly and gently. He didn't want to hurt her, he wanted her first time to be special and it was.

They were pretty full on after that night. They saw each other more and more. He was planning to ask her to marry him. The money he'd been saving from his card games was to buy a ring, but he wanted to do things properly, he was planning to ask her mum for her hand. He'd never felt like this about any girl.

Chapter 2

October 1955

Zella and Patsy were playing the new rock and roll record that everyone was going mad over, *Change her Mind* by Eddie Dee, while they got ready to go out. Patsy was dancing round the bedroom while Zella put her 'think dramatic' black make up on. Patsy always loved the way Zella made her eyes up. Florence, on the other hand, thought it was far too much make up.

"Will you do my eyes like that, Zella?"

"Yeah… If you want me to."

"Yes I do, I do."

"Are you going somewhere nice with George?"

"No… I have finished with him once and for all."

"Have you? …because you have this crush?"

"Ohhhh Zella, you should see him, or maybe not!" She giggled.

As Zella painted her eyes, Patsy stared up at her. "You are so pretty Zella, why don't you have a boyfriend?"

"How do you know I haven't?"

"Zella Russell...Have you?"

"No... "

Zella was meeting her friends Cynthia and Dolly at the *Motive* dance hall for a rock n roll night. She wasn't seeing Alden as he was working late then meeting up with some of his friends,

Patsy was meeting her friend Mary and some others at the bowling alley. They'd had a few games when Patsy looked over at the refreshment bar and there, standing tall with quiffed black hair stood the man of her dreams. She'd bumped in to him a week ago in the café and she had the biggest crush on him. She was a little more forward than Zella and didn't think twice about going after what she wanted. She sauntered over to the bar, looking him up and down.

"Hi..."

"Hi there..."

"What's your name?"

"What's yours?"

"Patsy..."

"Well... Patsy, nice to meet you."

"You haven't told me your name"

He smiled shaking his head, then one his mate shouted at him.

"Magnet... Come on!"

"Magnet? That's your name...? Magnet?" She repeated, staring straight into those big grey eyes of his.

He smiled and told her politely he had to go but it was very nice meeting her. She watched him walk over to his friends before Mary ran up asking what she was doing talking to men she didn't know.

"I'm going to marry him, Mary."

"Yep... course you are."

"I'm telling you... I will."

Her mind was set, Magnet was the man for her and nothing was going to get in the way.

A couple of days later Patsy was walking along the canal back and there sat on the bench was the man of her dreams.

"Hello Magnet. That can't be your real name, can it?"

"Hello, Patsy. Well, that would be telling, wouldn't it?" He laughed.

"What are you doing here sat all alone?"

"Just sat having a peaceful minute."

"Oh... would you like some company?" Not missing an opportunity like this, she thought.

"Thank you, but no."

He knocked her ego for six in one fell swoop with his NO.

"I'll leave you to it then shall I?"

"Yes..."

"Bye then."

"Bye..."

Patsy walked away determined she wasn't going to look back after that However, she couldn't resist and as she turned she saw Magnet locked in a full on passionate kiss. The green eyed monster reared its ugly head, she felt so jealous. She could feel her teeth grinding together and her eyes narrowed with pure jealousy. Who was this women who had his undivided attention?

She watched them walk away hand in hand looking very in love. She did contemplate following but decided against it. All the way home she wondered who this women was. Was she his girlfriend. Worse still, was she his *wife*? Patsy vowed she would find out. If this woman was just his girlfriend she wouldn't get in Patsy's way, a wife would be more of a problem but Magnet would fall for her one way or another. Patsy couldn't believe she was even thinking how she could break up his marriage if there was one. She felt a little wicked but soon got over it, that's how much she wanted this man.

Each week she went to the bowling alley with Mary to see if he was there. He actually was most Friday nights and they had even become friendly, they would talk and he might buy her a drink. One particular Friday she had done everything she could to make sure he was going to notice her. She wore tight slacks and a tight sweater that showed her full assets.

"Hello…"

"Oh… Hi Patsy."

"What are your plans after here?"

"Hmm, I don't know. Why?"

"Well… maybe we could do something."

"Hmmm! I don't think so Patsy."

"Why not?"

"Patsy… Look … I *have* a girlfriend."

"Girlfriends come and go."

He laughed. "Oh Patsy… not this one… This one is for keeps!"

Patsy didn't want to hear that. Mary suggested she give up trying, he was in love so she was never going to get him. Patsy told Mary she would never give up, she was going to get him no matter what, and it would be the other girl that would be going.

"She's history!"

"How? You heard what he said."

"So fuckin what? I don't care what he said."

Mary laughed at her. "You're not in a romantic movie where girl meets boy and boy falls madly in love with her. You're living in fantasy land. I won't believe it 'til I see it."

Patsy told her she could laugh all she wanted.

Patsy watched him all night, she was transfixed on him and his every move. Mary told her she was like a love sick puppy. Even the rest of their friends told her to move on, that she was never going to get him. He seemed to be a one woman man. He was never seen flirting with women and, in fact, he had never even been seen with any woman.

Betty, one of Patsy's other friends suggested he might not like women at all and this lady he keeps mentioning may not exist. Patsy told her not be stupid, of course he liked women. After all, hadn't she seen him with this woman?

"Well… why have you never seen her then? You know, the love of his life. Why is she never with him?"

"I don't know, do I?"

"I'm just saying."

Mary nodded her head in agreement with Betty.

"Ohhhhh… don't you start, Mary."

"Betty has a point."

"I saw him with a women, OK? Now can we please change the subject?"

Next morning, Patsy was in the foulest mood. First she was late up then at the breakfast table she slammed her cup down and toyed with her breakfast, moving it round and round in circles.

"Patsy! Stop playing with your food!"

"I'm not" she snapped

"Don't take that tone with me young lady"

To make matters worse, Zella was unbelievably cheerful.

"*Good* morning."

"Morning, my dear."

Patsy huffed and puffed, irritated at how Zella was so cheerful, right now she was possibly the happiest person in the world.

"What's wrong with you?"

"Nothin…"

"Noth*ing*… Patsy." Florence corrected her.

"Nothing… Zella… NOTHING!"

"I'm warning you, Patsy." Florence scolded.

Patsy left the table and put her cardigan on, "I'm off to work now."

"You better come back in better mood, Patsy Russell!" Florence shouted after her.

Patsy wasn't much better when she got to work. Even poor old Fred got an earful when she got his tea wrong, which incidentally was her fault, but what really upset her was when George appeared.

"Hi Patsy."

"What do you want?" She snapped unpleasantly.

"I want to see if you have a break coming up… I wanted to talk to you."

"What about?"

"Not here."

"Lonnie, can I have my break?" She shouted over her shoulder.

"Patsy, it's only early yet."

"I know… but *please*."

"OK…

Patsy grabbed her cigarettes and stepped outside with George.

"Now what do you want?" and she lit a cigarette, blowing a big puff of smoke into the air.

George nearly choked as the smoke headed his direction.

"Why don't you want to see me anymore?" He spluttered as he got a mouthful of Patsy's smoke.

"Because I don't."

"Well… at least give me a reason."

She explained that she had simply gone off him but that wasn't good enough for George and he kept asking for a better reason. That had sounded a good enough reason for Patsy. She was trying to be nice about it, but he pressed and pressed so she gave him with both barrels, as blunt as she could be.

"You're *boring,* that's why."

"Boring?

"Yes and, furthermore, I have met someone else'"

"I thought we would get married someday."

"George, I wouldn't marry you if you were the last man on earth. Can you image my life, it would be so tedious, and I'd be tearing my hair out!" She was on a roll until George put his hand in the air stopping her.

"I get the picture. You don't need to say any more, I will not bother you again" Then he walked away and never turned back

She thought she might have gone just a tad overboard, and was cruel even. But he did ask!

Later that day, who should drop in for a cup of tea and a bite to eat but Magnet and Snippet, a mate. The frown she had been wearing suddenly disappeared. Lonnie couldn't believe the change in her mood.

"Uhhhh… I'll never understand women!" He mumbled, heading back to the kitchen to get Magnet and Snippet a bowl of stew he'd talked them in to having.

"Good afternoon, Magnet."

"Hi… Patsy"

"Hi, Patsy." Snippet said.

Patsy didn't take any notice of him though, she was focused completely on Magnet. She asked him again for his real name but he just simply laughed. After eating their stew and crispy cob they went on their way.

Patsy was in a better mood for the rest of the day, she simply had to get that man. When she got home that evening her mother asked if her mood had improved and whatever had put her in such a bad mood, she had been positively awful that morning.

"I'm sorry, Mum. George and I have broken up once and for all now."

"Is this to do with this new young man you've met? George is a lovely man"

"Yes he is… but he's not the man for me."

"Ohhhh… Patsy, I hope this young man you've met doesn't break your heart."

"He won't, Mum."

"I still want to meet him."

"And you will."

Chapter 3

Alden had gone to meet Zella in the café, their usual place. She was running a little late and Alden must have had three cups of tea by the time she arrived.

"I thought you had changed your mind."

"I'm sorry… I just had to finish putting some new dresses out. I'm here now, were you missing me?"

"Yes…"

"Shall we get a pot of tea?"

Alden laughed.

"What…?"

"Nothing."

"Let's be devils, order afternoon tea."

The waitress brought a stand with sandwiches and cakes on it and they ordered a pot of tea, nothing extravagant mind but nice all the same. They made small talk while they ate then Alden enquired when Zella's next day off would be.

"Why?"

"I thought we could go to Cleethorpes for a day out."

"Oooo… that sounds good."

"Well… day off?"

"As it happens, my day off is Friday."

"This… Friday?"

"Yes, I haven't had a Friday off for weeks"

"Friday it is then. I'll get the car from my buddy."

"The... car? I thought you had a car?"

He explained that he and his friend shared the car, it was cheaper to share than have one each.

Zella side eyed him. "I see…"

Alden laughed, totally amused by her face.

"Don't laugh at me, Mister."

"Or…?"

"Or I will have to smother you in kisses."

"Well, in that case…"

He laughed and move closer to Zella to kiss her and she kissed him back .

"I like that." He said.

"What…?"

"Your sweet lips on mine." As he sat staring at her. "You are the most beautiful girl I've ever seen."

"Aww… you big softie." She smiled.

After they had finished afternoon tea they had a stroll, hand in hand along the canal, stopping every now and then for a kiss and a cuddle. They were so happy, nothing could ever spoil this.

Friday

Come Friday they set off to Cleethorpes. It wasn't a long drive, just about an hour or so away. After finding a parking spot, they headed down to the beach and the funfair. There was big wheel and a helter skelter. They had a paddle in the sea and then made their way to the tea room. Alden bought two bottles of elderberry juice and asked the lady if he could take the sandwiches out with him and some cake to go with it. He wanted to take Zella out on the boating lake and have a sort of picnic.

They spent about an hour on the lake before Alden started messing around rocking the boat

"You are going tip us up!"

So he did it even more to get a reaction from Zella, rocking the boat from side to side.

"Tip us up, Alden, and we will be getting in your car all wet and that means wet seats."

"We'll have to take our clothes off then."

"Oh... I see!" Zella laughed.

Alden rowed back toward the café for well-needed cup of tea. Zella had had the best day. The lady in the café watched as they drank their tea looking lovingly into each other's eyes. She figured they had just got married.

"Why do you think that?" The other girl asked.

"I don't know... they look so in love."

"You don't have to be married to be in love. Besides, she has no wedding ring on."

"Ohhhh... I don't know. But it's nice to see how in love they are."

She hoped they would stay just as in love as they were today. As they were leaving the tea room she shouted a good bye to them. They waved cheerfully at her and said good bye before making their way back home.

A week later Alden took Zella to Manchester to see *Alvin Preston, Springfield Silver* and *Lucky Arrow*. She had got Cynthia to tell her mum a little white lie, asking her to say she was stopping with her for the night so she and Alden could spend the night together.

The rock and roll concert hall the place was packed. Well, after all, they were all there to see the fabulous Alvin Preston. All the girls loved him and the guys wanted to be him. Alden and Zella danced till they dropped. By the end of the night they couldn't dance any more.

They strolled back to the boarding house. As they got to their room, Zella was suddenly a little nervous. Even though they had made love before it was always in the back of his car, she had never been naked in front of him

"I'll close my eyes if you want me to."

"I'm sorry… I know it silly but…"

"Shhhhh … It's alright… I understand." He interrupted her gently, placing his finger over her lips.

Alden covered his eyes while she undressed quickly and snuck underneath the blankets. He was less modest and took everything off where he stood.

"That's really not fair."

"What …?" She asked.

"You watched me!" He laughed.

He jumped into bed. They smiled at each other, then he kissed her gently. His lips were so soft, his fingers gently pushed her hair back as he softly caressed her face, trailing down her neck to her breasts, down to her navel. All the while, he was kissing her passionately. She arched her back with delight, she love the way he touched her. He made her feel so special, as if she was the only women in the world, he moved between her thighs in to her moving slowly teasing her. She gripped him tightly him as he moved in rhythm with her. He was a generous lover and always made sure she was satisfied as well.

The next morning they went down for their breakfast then caught the train back home. Zella was sure her mother would know she hadn't been with Cynthia and would find out the truth about what she really had been doing. She was so relieved when she realised she had got away with it, she really wasn't in the habit of lying to her mother.

Peggy noticed a change in Zella, she was so much happier than she normally was, and it all must be down to the young handsome reporter. It was nice to see. Zella was such a nice young woman, she deserved to be happy and in love. Peggy was really happy for her .

The weeks rolled by, until Alden was informed he was going to Blackpool to cover a story at the Pleasure Beach. He asked Zella if she would like to go with him but she told him she couldn't tell her mother she was staying with Cynthia again.

"It's just for the day."

"Oh…well, in that case… I'll have to ask Peggy if she'll swap my day in."

Alden smiled, "Then you'll come?"

Zella giggled excitedly. "Yes... who wouldn't want to go to Blackpool for the day?"

When they arrived in Blackpool, Alden quickly covered his story on the new attractions at the Pleasure Beach, it only took about an hour.

Now he and Zella could spend the rest of the day together. First, they went on the Big Dipper and the Velvet Coaster, then tried the other attractions. He even won her a prize on the Coconut Shy.

"I'm hungry. What about you, Zella?"

"I'm surprised you can eat anything after going on the whip."

He strolled over to the stall across from them and bought candy floss.

"Try this...?"

He placed a small piece of candy floss between his fingers and proceeded to feed Zella with it. She gently nibbled the candy from his fingers.

"Hmmm... that's so nice." She said, licking the sugary floss from her lips.

Alden watched her intently and got a warm feeling in the pit of his stomach.

"That was very sexy, Miss Russell."

"What, this?" She said, smiling as she did it again.

"Yes... you're teasing me."

"I'm teasing you." She giggled.

He rolled his eyes and smiled warmly at her, taking her hand.

"Come on! Let's get something to eat."

They jumped on a tram and made their way to central pier and grabbed a bite to eat at the shellfish bar and got a hot chocolate. They talked about him meeting her mum, he had something very important to ask her. By now, Zella agreed to introducing Alden, she thought it was the right time.

"That's settled then."

"I will get it all organised."

"What's to organise?" He asked.

"You don't know my mother. Trust me, we have to organise this!" She laughed

"OK …"

"Really, she will need to make afternoon tea and she will ask you a hundred and one questions."

He laughed, totally taken up with her.

"Come, lets go for a stroll."

Hand in hand they strolled along the promenade, they even had a donkey ride and paddled in the sea. They had had such a wonderful day.

When Zella had got back home she told her mother she had met a young man and wanted to bring him home to meet her. Florence looked at Zella and smiled.

"Yes, of course. I would love to meet your young man."

Zella was really pleased at her mother's reaction and felt more at ease. It did, however, remind Florence about Patsy's young man and she told Zella she would sort it all out but would she mind if she met Patsy's young man first, as Patsy had been putting her off for weeks. Besides, Florence knew Zella was the sensible one out of the two of them.

Zella was more than happy for Patsy to bring her boyfriend home first, mainly so she could see what their mother's reaction was going to be like. Patsy was pleased too.

"Thank you… Zella… Mum won't let up until she meets Magnet."

"Magnet? What kind of name is Magnet?"

"It's a nickname, I think."

"So what's his real name?"

"Hmmm. I don't know"

Florence chirped up, "You still don't know this young man's name?"

"I swear mum has ears like a bat."

"Yes, and I have eyes like a hawk too."

Florence demanded that Patsy bring this young man home for afternoon tea the next day at 3.30pm. She expected him to be there on the dot.

"Woe betide you if he doesn't come."

"But mum…"

"But Mum, *nothing*."

Patsy had jumped the gun a little. She had made their relationship out to be a little more than it actually was. She didn't quite know how to get him to come for tea, she hadn't even been out on a date with him! Why would he want to come for afternoon tea? She had to do something and fast.

When she bumped into him and Snippet that evening, she asked him straight out.

"Will you come to tea?" She blurted out.

"Are you always this forward?"

"Yep."

"Why?"

"Why...? What?"

"Why would I come to afternoon tea, Patsy?"

He didn't realise just how big a crush she had on him. He had never encouraged her in any way, if anything it was the opposite. Patsy, however, was the most forward and boisterous one of Zella and herself.

"Don't laugh... my mum wants to meet you."

"Why?"

"She just does."

"For what reason, Patsy...?"

"I sort of gave her the impression that you were my boyfriend..."

"Why?"

"Please, don't be mad with me."

He burst out laughing, "OK... but you must tell her I'm not your boyfriend."

"Why is that funny?"

"It is... I told you"

"Yeah ...yeah ...yeah, you have a girlfriend"

Pasty told him he could be her boyfriend if he wanted to be.

"You're too young for me. You're a child. How old are you, anyway?"

"Do I look like a child to you?"

She moved her hands seductively down her body show her curves off. Snippet gulped and swallowed deeply, his eyes bulging out of their sockets.

"OK, not a child…" He said, taking a deep breath, "but too young for me."

"I'm eighteen… how old are you?"

"Patsy, I'm in my twenties and too old for you and that's that."

Patsy didn't like that and stormed off moodily. She suddenly remembered she had to get him to her house otherwise she would be in so much trouble with her mum. She turned around and yelled.

"My mum is expecting you tomorrow at 3.30pm. Please don't be late." And gave him the address.

He smiled to himself, "Crazy girl."

"How do you do it? You get all the ladies. You have one on the go and now another one's pining all over you." Snippet asked.

"I dunno… pure animal magnetism?" He laughed.

"You are one lucky son of a gun."

"I know…"

"But seriously… going to tea. I didn't think you did tea." Snippet laughed

"Hmmm, Yeah… I'll do her this favour then she needs to tell her mum we are *not* stepping out"

Snippet chuckled. "Come on, we're going to be late."

They made their way to work for the team meeting and rostered assignments.

At the Russell household, Florence had set about making some bread, a Victoria Sponge and her own jam. Zella was helping with the preparations. In truth, she was quite excited to meet Patsy's beau.

Patsy, however, was rather nervous, so nervous she couldn't sleep. Later that night she woke Zella up so she could talk to her

"Patsy… it's 3 o'clock – go back to sleep!" Zella was so weary, she'd had a long day at the boutique and she'd helped with everything for tomorrow.

"Zella, please wake up."

"OK, what is it?"

"What if mum doesn't like him?"

"Uhhhh Patsy, I'm sure our mother will love him." Wanting to go back to sleep, she turned over

"Zell…*please*

"Patsy… you're driving me nuts."

"I love him so much, I need mum to like him, and you know what she's like/"

Zella got out of bed and moved over to Patsy.

"You really do love this man don't you?"

"With all my heart, Zella. You have to help me with mum, you have to be on my side with this, OK?"

"It 'll be fine. Trust me, I'm your big sister, now will you *please* go to sleep?"

Zella got back into bed and was out like a light.

Chapter 4

The next day Magnet arrived at Patsy's house promptly at 3.30. Florence open the door and greeted him.

"Hello… Magnet, I presume? Patsy's young man. That can't be your real name."

"Hello… Alden Pearce" He took Florence's outstretched hand and gently kissed it.

"Come on in. I'm Mrs Russell, Patsy's mother."

"Thank you, Mrs Russell."

'Mrs Russell?' He thought, alarm bells going off in his head. No, no, no… this could not be a coincidence, he had such a bad feeling about this. He was about to tell Mrs Russell that he wasn't Patsy's young man at all when Patsy herself bolted down the stairs to greet him.

"Magnet… Mum and Zella have laid on a lovely spread." Shouted Patsy.

"Patsy, don't shout like that, it's not ladylike." Florence said sternly.

Alden's mind was working overtime. 'Zella?' It couldn't be *his* Zella. He was praying it wasn't his Zella but how many Zellas could there be? This was bad, really bad.

"Who's Zella?" He asked

"My sister…"

Zella suddenly appeared at the top of the stars and started to saunter down. A look of horror swept across his face when he saw her. It *was* his Zella. Ohhhh noooo this could not be.

When Zella saw Alden she gasped with sheer shock. She stared at him, looking him straight in the eyes. Florence saw the look on both their faces and suddenly felt uneasy about all of this.

"Meet Magnet… Zella"

"Alden is my name… but you…"

She quickly interrupted him.

"Nice to meet you, Alden." Her voice was icy cold.

A puzzled look swept across Alden's face. Florence suggested that they go into the lounge where they sat and talked for a while. Instead of Florence, though, it was Zella who fired questions at him here, there and everywhere. Florence wondered what had got into her even though she had an idea or thought she had. Even Patsy wondered what on earth had got into Zella, she wasn't like that normally.

"Patsy, come along help with the tea."

"Oh Mum… ugh."

"Patsy… you have a guest. Zella can keep Alden company while we are in the kitchen."

As soon as they disappeared from sight, Alden looked at Zella.

"Zella what are you doing?" He whispered.

"I live here, what are you doing?"

"This is not …."

She cuts him off. "I see what this is and we will not be seeing each other again, Alden"

"Zella this isn't…"

"Don't… say another word!"

"We need to talk."

"No, there will be no talking." Alden had never seen her so cold.

"We have to talk about this, Zella."

"No we don't. It's all very clear to me."

"No… it's not let me explain."

"Nothing to explain, Magnet."

Alden was just about to tell her that all this was just a mistake, when Patsy and Florence came back in with a tray with bread and a pot of home mad jam. There was also a lovely Victoria Sponge and a pot of tea.

Florence asked him all about his job and his family. He told her he didn't have a family, they had been killed in the war and he had been a evacuee, he'd been evacuated to Wales with a host family.

"I'm very sorry Alden, that must have been very hard, not to mention distressing."

"Yes it was, so I've had to make my own way in life."

"That is very sad."

He was trying desperately trying to tell Florence that Patsy was just a friend, but every time he was about to say something Patsy interrupted him.

Zella tried desperately not to make eye contact with Alden all afternoon, she avoided it at all costs. He had broken her heart in to a million pieces, she had to fight her tears back. She had never been in love before. He was her first, her first lover, how could he have done this to her?

Patsy looked so happy she didn't want to spoil that for her. She loved her sister and would do anything for her, even if that meant giving up the man she loved. Alden was desperate to explain but he couldn't do it there.

"I must head off now, I have an assignment later today."

"How exciting... It's been lovely meet you, Alden."

"Thank you for inviting me.

"You're welcome.... Patsy, show Alden to the door."

Patsy walked him to the door. Alden looked back to see if Zella was there. He knew she was angry, but once he had explained she would see what a mistake this all was

"You need to tell your mother we are not a couple Patsy"

"I will"

"*Now*, Patsy. *Now...*"

Patsy felt a little upset that Alden still felt that way, he'd had managed to upset two women today through no fault of his own.

Zella, meanwhile, rushed up stairs rather quickly. She didn't even help Florence with the pots which were so unlike her. She cried and cried silently in the bathroom. She made herself sick she had sobbed so much. She couldn't catch her breath, she couldn't believe this was happening. After she had given her self to him he had told to her loved her he had even told her he wanted to spend the rest of his life with her.

Her head was spinning as her mind went over and over everything. He must have thought he would have some fun with her little sister first. She was so hurt and then hurt quickly turned to anger, she wasn't thinking clearly. She would never forgive him for this, although she had learnt a valuable lesson.

The next day Zella went into work but she wasn't herself all day. Peggy ended up putting her in the stock room sorting out all the new designs, putting them on hangers ready to go out on to the shop floor. She knew there was something wrong with Zella, she was always so happy and focused, but not today, she was not with it at all, so she sent her on an early lunch. Alden was waiting for her round the corner near the café.

"Zella…"

Zella looked at him and walked straight past him. He had to run to catch up with her and he grabbed her by the hand.

"Zella… *talk* to me."

"Let go!" She was so cold.

"I want to explain."

"I don't want to hear it… Now go away!"

She pulled out of his grip and walked away. Alden decided to wait until after she finished work to try again and he hung around all day. After she finished work she spotted him lurking so she walked the other way. He ran after her shouting her name.

"Go away, Alden."

"No… I need to explain…"

She stopped in her tracks and shouted at him. "Were you seeing my sister?"

"Yes, but not *that* way…"

She abruptly interrupted him, cutting him off in mid-sentence. "Then we don't need to talk again."

"Zella… please listen…"

"We never need to discuss this ever again. Patsy will never know about us. If you tell her, I will never forgive you, Alden."

She walked away. Alden went after her and pulled her back, *"Zella…"*

Zella told him to release his grip which he did, reluctantly. She was so stern, cold. How could she be so cold? She refused to listen. She had said she loved him, why wouldn't she listen? He just wanted to grab her and make her listen to him.

She desperately needed to get away from him and began to walk faster, tears rolling down her face. He finally stopped and watched her walk away.

Alden tried several times after that to talk to her but she still wouldn't listen to him. Patsy, however ,was still chasing after him none the wiser. He wasn't in the mood for Patsy and her silly crush, he needed to talk to Zella.

"Hi Alden"

"Just leave me alone."

"Why, what's wrong?"

"Patsy, just go away …go play with your friends."

"Play with my friends?"

She didn't like that and stormed off in a huff. She turned back and told him she wouldn't give up and that he *would* fall in love with her, then headed back over to her friends.

44

Alden didn't think any more about it. His thoughts were only for Zella and how to get her to talk to him, all he was interested in was how to get her to believe him. He thought Patsy would simply get over her crush and it would be a new boy next week.

Zella was down for weeks. Cynthia and Dotty were worried about her and suggested they went out for the day to try cheer her up. Zella told them she didn't want to do anything but they insisted they were all going to Cleethorpes for the day.

"No, I don't want to."

"Well, we've got to do *something*. We're worried about you."

"Come on, let's have a pot of tea in the café." Cynthia suggested.

Zella sat down with Cynthia while Dotty ordered the tea.
"Zella, what's the matter?"

"Nothing…"

"We know there's something wrong, please tell us."

Zella put her head down just as Dotty come back with the tea.

"Zella?"

"…I fell in love."

"For someone who's fallen in love you don't look very happy." Cynthia said, stating the obvious.

"It's over… He hurt me with someone close to me."

"Who?" Dotty asked.

"Who?… Doesn't matter."

Zella looked up at them, tears forming in her eyes. As they begin to fall, they both took her hands and moved their heads closer to hers, trying desperately to console her.

"I loved him with all my heart and he has broken it into tiny pieces, as if it was just one of those things. How could he do that?"

"You'll get over it and he will be a distant memory." Dotty swore.

"No... Dotty. I will never get over this, he was the love of my life, and I will never love any man like I loved him."

Cynthia and Dotty didn't know what to say after that. Whoever this man was had really torn her apart.

For weeks she was weepy and distant. Peggy knew it had something to do with Alden but she really didn't want to pry. She looked so sad and Peggy tried desperately to cheer her up with her witty comments, but nothing seemed to work. Zella finally mentioned that she couldn't stay there any longer and started looking for work out of Chesterfield. Peggy didn't want to lose Zella, she had not only became a valued employee but a close friend too.

Chapter 5

Zella couldn't stand it anymore, all Patsy could talk about was Alden, Alden *this* Alden *that*. She would silently cry herself to sleep. She couldn't keep pretending any more. It broke her heart every time Patsy mentioned Alden's name so she decided to just move away and forget all about him. She took the train to Stoke on Trent and managed to get herself a job as a seamstress in a clothes factory for Carlos Nomikos. His foreman had a friend who rented rooms so he helped her with a room. Only then could she tell her mum she had got a new job.

She had let Peggy and her two best friends know that she was leaving and she promised she would let them know how she was getting along. Maybe they could visit her when she was settled in.

Florence wasn't too sure about her moving all the way to Stoke on her own but Zella reassured her that she would be all right. She wanted to get herself a career in fashion and this was the only way. Florence knew there was something else and she knew it had something to do with Alden

"I'm still worried about you being in Stoke alone, Zella."

"I know… but I will be fine."

"I know. You're a sensible young woman and you need to spread your wings."

"Yes I do, I'll be fine, I promise"

"Well I want to come to see you when you settle"

"Of course, mum. I want you to visit."

Within a matter of weeks, Zella moved to Stoke and made the little bedsit her own. She thought this would be the best way to get over Alden and move on.

Alden still didn't know Zella had left. He had been in Scotland covering a story about a shopkeeper and his success as he had opened a third branch. When he got back he bumped in to Patsy at the bowling alley and casually asked her about Zella.

"Zella has moved."

"Moved… where?"

"Stoke… Why are so keen to know about my sister?"

"I hadn't seen her around… That's all. What's she doing in Stoke?"

"She's finding her career. Where have you been anyway?"

"Scotland… Glasgow, actually."

"And how is that girlfriend of yours?"

Alden wasn't sure how to answer so he just changed the subject .

"Oooo… *Trouble in paradise?*"

"No…"

"Why have I never seen you with her?"

"She's busy."

"Hmmm." She mumbled.

"What…?"

"*Interesting.*"

"Why is that interesting?" He snarled. Patsy wasn't the person he wanted to see right now, he was in no mood for her at all.

She smiled, "It just *is*, that's all"

Alden told her he had to go and would see her around. Patsy by now had the idea in her head that he was lying about his girlfriend. Perhaps he didn't really have one, like Betty had said, or maybe he was seeing a married women. It would explain why he was never out in public with her. *'Yes, yes. That's it!'* She thought.

Alden wanted to find Zella, maybe she would talk to him now. The following week he asked Stan if he could cover an upcoming story in Stoke. Stan agreed and gave him two day's expenses for a boarding house and food. Alden arrived in Stoke and got straight to work on the story.

Over the two days, he looked everywhere he could for Zella but Stoke was a big place. It was like looking for a needle in a hay stack, *where was he to start?* He looked round a number of shops and cafés but she was nowhere to be found. After story was finished and he couldn't justify staying any longer, he went back to Chesterfield, very deflated. He realised he had never loved any one the way he loved Zella.

When he got back home, it soon became apparent that Betty couldn't have been more wrong about him. He *did* like girls. In fact he'd gone into overdrive, determined to live up to his nickname, ladies to left and ladies to the right, he was seen every night with a different one. Even Snippet couldn't keep up with him.

"What's with you lately?"

"Nothing.... Why?"

"You're chasing skirt like it's gone out of fashion."

"I'm having fun, nothing is worth worrying about."

"What do ya mean?"

"Derick, let's get out of Chesterfield."

"Why...? I like it here I want to stay, belong somewhere instead of moving around like we have been. What is wrong with you?"

"Nothing... stay it is, then."

"Alden, are you in trouble?"

"No..."

"Well why do you want to move away, you were happy enough a few weeks ago what's changed? Is this to do with a girl?"

"No... It's all good."

A new day

As it turned out, Stan gave Alden and Derick a new assignment which would take them to the Isle of Man to cover the TT Races. Derick was really looking forward to it.

It was the start of a whirlwind few weeks.

They got to the Isle of Man for the start of the races on what was one of the most dangerous racing circuits in the world.

Public roads would be closed and they would be racing the Clypse Course, this year with a full grid. Derick was in his element and he and Alden were privileged to meet former champions Ivan Palmer and Don Dixon JR, still racing as well as ever.

On the second week they got talking to Clive Berry. He loved speed and he would travel to as many places as he could to see races, motorcycle races in particular. Derick assumed he was a successful businessman or something. Money just didn't seem to be an issue for him. Alden and Derick spent their evenings with him. After all, he knew all the best places to go.

The following week they headed to the Channel Islands, to Jersey to cover the Battle of the Flowers parade. Although it had declined during World War II, a local businessman thought it would be good for tourists so they brought it back once again.

When they finally reported back to Stan he told them to head to Liverpool as there was a new pop music sensation, called 'The Reptiles', and he wanted them to be the first paper to report on them. When Alden told him they were heading to Liverpool, Derick got really excited. He'd heard about The Reptiles and thought if they were lucky they might even get to see the legendary Kitty Laine.

By the time their train got into the station they were so tired they just wanted to get to their boarding house and sleep, they went out like a light. Derick dreamt about the beautiful Kitty Laine, her beautiful red hair and those long, shapely legs. Next morning he woke up feeling refreshed and ready for the day ahead.

"Are you ready to see *The Reptiles* and, of course, the glamorous Kitty?"

"Derick... Kitty Laine might not even be there."

"Don't spoil this for me, she'll be there! Oh ye of little faith."

Alden chuckled. "She ain't gonna even look your way, pal."

They had arranged to interview the band at the Rock n Roll Den although the man at the door was reluctant to let them in until Derick told him they were press and he quickly changed his mind. As they made their way in, they could hear the music blasting out.

"That's got to be *The Reptiles*..."

"Yep... I would definitely say it is with that jazzy blues blasting out."

They finished their interview and Derick snapped more than enough pictures, he got some great shots. They were just packing up their equipment when Kitty Laine sauntered in. Derick got more than excited but, like Alden had said ,she didn't even know he was there. He never got near her and she never even looked his way, not even a glance. He was so disappointed, he had wanted so much to meet her.

On their way back to Chesterfield, Derick was quiet and Alden asked him what was wrong, as if he didn't know.

"She didn't even look my way."

"I did tell you..."

"It's not just Kitty Laine though, is it?"

"Well, who else are talking about?"

"That Patsy girl."

"Oh don't even mention her name, Derick."

"Why… she likes you."

"I met someone… someone I really cared for and Patsy has ruined that for me and that special someone doesn't want to ever see me again."

"Alden, I thought when you told Patsy about a girlfriend you were making it sound more serious than it actually was."

"I've never felt this way about anyone before. You know me, hence the nickname, *Magnet*, huh."

"Why don't you tell this girl… that it was…" He hesitated momentarily.

"It doesn't matter now, she wants nothing to do with me."

"But…"

Alden interrupted him. " I don't want to talk about this again, and as far as Patsy is concerned, I'm not interested and she doesn't need to know anything."

Derick understood and never said another word.

They got back and said they would meet up later. On his way home, Derick bumped in to Patsy. He said hello to her but she barely even noticed him.

"Patsy…"

"Ohhhh, Snippet. Where is Magnet? I mean Alden."

"Magnet…?"

"Yeah…"

"Is that all your bothered about? No *'Hello Snippet'*? Why don't you let it go? He's not interested, he's in love with someone else, just *stop!*"

Then he walked away with his head down. Patsy wondered what had gotten into him, he wasn't normally that rude.

Chapter 6

Zella had been in Stoke for almost a year, going to work then making her way home. She didn't really know anyone so she didn't socialise very much, she worked on her designs most nights. She loved working for Carlos Nomikos. She had settled in to her new job and had made her bedsit very cosy.

Reg, Carlos's foreman had noticed how hard Zella worked and he also noticed how much she liked drawing.

"What are you drawing Zella?"

"Oh nothing… just something I like doing."

"Are they designs for clothes?" He asked, curiously.

"Yes, I make my own clothes"

"Can I see?"

She handed them over to him.

"Wow… Zella, these are great. Can you make some up and bring them in? Carlos is here tomorrow, he will love these."

"Really… do you think so?"

After work, Zella headed home and started working up two dresses: one a full circle skirt dress and the other was a party dress, sexy and elegant.

She was so caught up in it that she worked all through the night. Meanwhile, Reg had told Carlos about Zella's designs and he was very intrigued.

"She has got something, Carlos. Her designs are out of this world, nothing like we have seen before."

"I want to see them"

"I have asked her to make some things and bring them in tomorrow."

"Excellent."

Next morning, Zella had just finished the last dress when she looked over at the clock. *'Oh Hell,'* she thought. *'I'd better get moving'*. She washed quickly and painted on her happy face. She was so tired but if this paid off it would be worth it.

"You look tired. Have you been working on these all night, Zella?"

"Yes."

"Come with me."

Zella followed Reg into Carlos's office where he was sat in a big comfy chair with his feet up on the desk, blowing cigar smoke out of his mouth.

"Carlos, this is Zella."

"Hello, my darling" and he looked her up and down.

"Look at these, Carlos …show him, Zella."

She took the first dress out of the bag and Carlos' eyes widened. Then she took the second dress out and he jumped to his feet.

"You designed these and made them?"

"Yes, sir."

"Do you have any more?"

Zella nodded.

"Show me … show me!"

Zella took the sketchpad with all her designs in from her bag and handed it to him. A big smile swept across his face.

"Wow, these are amazing, Zella! Will you have dinner with me and my wife tonight, so we can discuss your future?"

"I would love to."

Zella's career took off after that evening. She became one of Carlos's designers and she produced more ideas. Quickly, she became his top designer.

As well as Stoke, he had other factories, one in Chesterfield and one near London. This was a bigger outlet and he decided that Zella should work out of there so he drove her down to look it over.

"Well, Zella?"

"Uh… It's *big*."

"I want you here."

"Here?"

"Yes… What do you think?"

"Hmmm…. Yes I would love to"

Carlos smiled. "Good, we will find you a place here."

Carlos had a friend who soon arranged a place for Zella to live. It was more rent but it was much better and bigger. Carlos figured she would need the extra space for her creations.

She sent a letter to her mum to tell her the news, Florence was excited but also worried about her daughter being in London on her own. Being in Stoke on her own had been bad enough but London, that was even bigger. She knew Zella was a sensible young woman but she was still worried.

Zella told her mum that she wanted her and Patsy to come and spend Christmas with her in Stoke and Florence told her they would be there. Meanwhile Zella got in to full production with her new designs. Christmas was just round the corner, no time for parties. She had the idea to make Patsy's gift this year, she had made her a swing dress to show off her stunning curves. Carlos thought the design was sensational and asked if she would consider letting him put it into production.

"Sure, I don't mind at all"

"That's great. You have a real gift, Zella."

"Thank you"

"I'm serious, sales have soared since you became our designer."

"We have to keep it up…"

"Yes, but I know you can do it."

Christmas

Seeing she had her mum and sister coming over, Zella thought she better do some Christmas shopping, she really wanted it to be special.

She had bought her mum a pearl necklace with matching bracelet. They weren't expensive but it's the thought that counts, that's what Florence had always told her . She also bought a small tree but waited till her mum and Patsy arrived to decorate it. She thought it would be nice to trim the tree together like they used to.

As it got closer to Florence and Patsy arriving, she bought everything to make a traditional Christmas dinner she really wanted to make it like being at home. She was very excited and emotional when her mum and sister finally arrived, she had missed them both very much. They were still hugging and crying when Carlos called round. He had brought her a Christmas hamper full of goodies.

"Thank you Carlos that was a considerate thing to do but I'm so sorry, I didn't buy you anything."

"That's alright, Zella."

"Let me introduce you… this is my mum and my sister."

"It's very nice to meet you both. You have a talented daughter, Mrs Russell."

"Yes, she's a very clever girl."

"She is indeed… Enjoy your Christmas, Ladies."

He turned to Zella. "I have a favour to ask of you, my dear."

"Yes… What is it?"

"I have to attend a Dinner party on New Year's Eve. Would you join my wife and myself…?"

"I would love to."

"I can introduce you to some important people too"

"That would great."

Patsy got it in her head that Carlos was interested in Zella. Why else would he want her to accompany him to a dinner party? She looked at Zella, raised her eyebrows and smiled. Zella shook her head and rolled her eyes.

"He's my boss and he is happily married and, furthermore, *she* will be there with us."

"I still think he likes you."

"Ohhhh... Patsy, you need to grow up!"

Patsy huffed and puffed and said that she would... if she was allowed to. Zella asked what she meant by that.

It seemed that after Zella had left home, their mother gone in to over-protective mode and now she might have to move out too.

"You *are* the youngest –she is bound to want to protect you."

"Zella, she treats me like a little girl"

"Well, you *are* her little girl."

"I need to spread my wings."

Zella did see Patsy's point and suggested that Florence loosen the apron strings a bit. Florence agreed but did point out that Patsy wasn't always as sensible as she was and that worried her

"Mum, she has to make her own way and you can be there if she makes a mistake."

"Listen to you!" She laughed.

They had a wonderful Christmas. It was nice being together but sadly it was soon time for Pasty and Florence to go back home to Derbyshire. Another Christmas had come and gone. Zella took then to the train station to see them off. Florence asked when she would move to London and Zella tells her that it will be after the festive holidays.

"Be careful in London, Zella, it's a big place." She said, kissing and hugging.

"Oh Mum, it's the same as anywhere."

"I know, but I do worry about you there on your own."

She kissed her mum and Pasty goodbye and waved them off then caught the bus back home. She got into her pyjamas, made herself some hot milk and listened to the radio while she relaxed in front of the fire and caught up on some reading.

New Year's Eve

New Year's Eve came and she wondered what she should wear for this dinner party Carlos was taking her to. Was she to dress up fancy or not? She decided to call him to ask so she made her way down the street to the telephone box on the corner. *RING, RING...* went the phone. Carlos answered in a deep voice.

"Hello?"

"Hello. It's Zella."

"Zella... are you ready for tonight?"

"Yes... but I was wondering to I need to dress up

"Yes Zella... dress up – wear one of your designs.

"OK."

"We'll pick you up at seven thirty sharp."

He was quite precise about the time, he was a stickler for punctuality. Zella went back to her flat and looked through all her designs and picked out a ruby red and silver toned dress. It had cropped sleeves, a high neck at the front and low v-neck at the back as it dropped to the knee.

She had the perfect shoes to go with it, they were silver ankle strap stilettos she'd bought before Christmas. With her shoulder bouffant hairpiece she created some height. She added her make up last. White eyeshadow with dramatic black eye liner and luscious red lips, she looked amazing.

When Miriam and Carlos picked her up, Miriam remarked on how stunning she was. Zella thanked her and repaid the compliment. As they pulled up Zella was astounded by the glamour of everyone entering the grand building. She had never seen anything so beautiful.

Zella and Miriam waited for Carlos to get drinks when a handsome young man appeared at her side. He looked very dashing with quiffed sandy hair and big brown eyes drawing her in as he stared at her.

"Hello." He said in a soft but strong voice.

"Hello."

"Are you here alone?"

"No... I'm with my Carlos Nomikos and his wife Miriam"

Miriam smiled.

"Oh I see...Carlos uhhhh. I believe he has found himself a shit hot designer. Excuse the language." He said apologetically as he took a long, drawn out drag on his cigarette before blowing the smoke into the air.

"Yes I've heard that too..." she giggled, looking at Miriam who gave her a little smirk.

"Yes, she is very good apparently."

"Really...?."

"Hello, Clive." A voice came from behind him

"Carlos, my man"

"I see you have met Zella..."

"*Zella* ... That's your name, that was my next question ... and what does *Zella* do?"

"Well... I'm a designer."

Clive smiled. "You are the shit hot designer aren't you?"

Zella gave a little giggle. "You said I was, so I must be."

"Clive, you must see her designs." Carlos said, stepping between them.

"I would love to."

"Clive's father founded *Sapphires*, one of the top clothes stores in London and he took over the business when his father retired."

Clive seemed to be very interested in Zella. He told her she needed to come to the store to show him her designs.

"Yes... I would like that."

"So, that's settled then."

Chapter 7

1956

1956 was approaching, then the clock suddenly struck twelve and everyone cheered and wished each other a happy new year. Clive had watched Zella all evening as she mingled with the other guests and he told Carlos he wanted to get to know her. He also asked him to arrange for her to come to Sapphires. His interest, however, lay in more than just seeing her designs.

When Carlos dropped her off he told her that Clive wanted her to show him her collection very soon. Her jaw dropped.

"Oh wow! That place is somewhere you dream of shopping."

"Yes... it's very big and Clive seems to like you."

Zella blushed. Carlos suggested she got in touch with him when the store opened after the holidays, she said she would call and arrange it.

Clive wasn't the only one that wanted to know all about Zella. Marcel de Fae was also very intrigued with Zella's designs and he told Carlos he also would like to see her collection. After he had seen them, though, he was unimpressed. He flicked though them muttering *"No, no, no… fastidieuses… même vieux, pas d' imagination."*

"*Boring… same old… no imagination…* Are you joking, Marcel?" Carlos said angrily.

"NO… No joke, Carlos."

"Well, Marcel… your loss."

"Bye, Mademoiselle Russell, *je ne reverrai pas.*"

"Bye, Monsieur De-Fae"

"Marcel… I think you're wrong and, furthermore, I think you *will* see her again."

After Marcel left Zella was heartbroken. She wasn't asking to be a top designer, even though it would be nice, she just simply had a passion for designing clothes and would like her name on her own range.

"Don't be downhearted, Zella."

"But… You heard what he said."

"Sure but I know you will catch someone's attention with your designs…He's plain wrong."

The following week, Zella went to went Sapphires expecting to hear more of the same, de Fae had really knocked her confidence. Clive had some tea brought in while he looked at her selection of designs then he asked if she would like a guided tour of the store.

"Oh yes… if you have the time"

"Yes… of course. You must let me give you the Sapphire tour."

The place was huge, she had never seen a department store this big before and it took quite some time to get round. Finally, Clive took her to the clothes department. She stood there with her mouth wide open, her eyes could hardly take it all in. She didn't know what to look at first.

"This is super."

"Glad you like it... it's now *your* section of clothes."

"Yes..." She waited with baited breath

"I'll buy them all."

"*Really...*" She gasped. She couldn't believe what she was hearing.

"There's just one condition..."

"And... what is this condition?"

"You have dinner with me tonight."

"That's bribery..."

"Yep..."

She agreed. "What time tonight?"

"Seven... but now we go for lunch"

She stood and looked at him "Lunch?"

"Yes ...lunch. You do eat lunch don't you?"

"Yes... but aren't you busy"

He shook his head smiling then took her hand and they made their way to his car, a flash Jaguar XK140 sports car. She was impressed, to say the least.

"Oh My... look at this car." She said, running her fingers over the bonnet.

"Do you like it?"

"Yes ..."

"It drives like a dream." He smiled proudly.

Over lunch Clive seemed transfixed by her, he stared at all the way through. It made her a little nervous but yet excited. After he dropped her off, he called into Carlos' office to put in a huge order for the whole of Zella's clothes range. After he'd gone, Carlos shouted for Zella to come up.

"You must have made a big impression on Clive Berry..." And he told her about Clive's order.

It was a big, very big, a very big order indeed. Carlos was over the moon. Zella went back to her desk and immediately phoned Clive.

"Oh, thank you so much for the order, Mr Berry."

"*Mr Berry?* That's my dad. Clive, please, *Clive* ..."

"Clive..."

"I can't wait for tonight."

"Why...?"

"Our dinner date. I felt lonely, I missed you after I left you," he said playfully. "but it's OK. I get to see you again tonight."

She laughed. "You are so sweet"

"Yep..."

"Modest too, I see." They both laughed in unison.

That evening he picked her up in a Mercedes-Benz 300SL. "

"Just how many cars do you have?" She asked curiously, staring at the car.

"I have just another one. I like fast cars... and beautiful women." He added.

"I bet you do, but one day some beautiful lady will steal your heart." She smiled

"She already has."

Zella blushed, she could feel her face go incredibly warm until it must have been beetroot red. She lowered her head to hide how red she had gone. Clive placed his fingers under her chin to lift her head back up.

"You are so beautiful."

"Please stop, I'm already beetroot red." She stammered

"Now I have found you, you can't leave me, I simply can't allow it."

Zella had been here before, she was very taken with Clive but she wanted to take this very slow. She had been hurt badly by Alden, she wasn't about to get hurt again.

He opened the car door for her like any gentleman would, then headed off to *Scorpions*, Clive liked fine food too it seems. She enjoyed being with Clive, he was so charming, so handsome and very witty. They talked and talked, they seemed to have a lot in common. He asked why she didn't have a boyfriend and she told him about Alden, that she'd had one it just hadn't worked out. She asked him the same question, why didn't he have a girlfriend.

"I have been waiting for you…"

"I see." She chuckled.

"I'm serious."

"Of course you are…"

Clive wanted to see Zella again. He was used to getting his own way and he wasn't taking no for an answer, As it happens she didn't say no. She liked him. She liked his sandy hair and rich, brown eyes, his chiselled chin and piano smile and he was witty and kind. She hadn't once thought about Alden since she met Clive.

❧ ☙

Out of the blue, Ruth Johnson popped in to see Carlos. They chit chatted for a while then Ruth noticed some sketches sticking out from under some paperwork on Carlos's desk. She teased them out with her finger.

"What are these?"

"They are designs"

"Let me look…"

Carlos showed her the top few and she asked who had designed them. Carlos told her him about Zella and asked if she would like to meet her. While Carlos was out of the office, Ruth had look at the other designs before something caught her eye, a trumpet scooped neck tulle, capped sleeve dress embellished with diamantés. The way Zella had designed it, the lace would simply shimmer. Ruth had to have this design so she took it from the pile and put it neatly in her bag. By this time, Carlos had found Zella as she was on her way back from the shop floor.

"Zella come, I have someone who would like to meet you."

Zella followed Carlos into his office and there, sat waiting patiently was Ruth.

"Pleased to meet you, Miss Russell"

"Ohhhh, Miss Johnson, it's a pleasure to meet you too, you have got some spectacular Designs."

Zella knew exactly who Ruth was, shed seen her in a trade magazine.

"Well, Ruth, what do you think of Zella designs?"

"They are good… but not for me."

Carlos was taken aback. She had seemed so enthusiastic earlier what had changed he didn't understand

"But you liked them earlier..."

"Yes... but then I had a closer look."

"I see..."

Zella thanked her for looking and Ruth wished her luck with her career then left. Carlos was still confused to the sudden change of heart, it was so disappointing.

As time went on Zella worked hard on her designs and had also been seeing a lot of Clive. He took her out almost every night, always somewhere different and fun. She told her mum all about him and, of course, she wanted to meet him. He had said they could take the day to go to Derbyshire but Zella wasn't sure about that and suggested that Florence and Patsy came to London to stay for a couple of days. Florence said that would be lovely. Patsy, however,wasn't keen. She didn't see why she had to go, she preferred to stay at home.

Florence insisted she was going and that was that.

A couple of day before they arrived, Clive arranged to spend the day with Zella, as he had planned to pop the question before her mum and sister arrived. He had decided to take her to Hyde Park.

The next day, he picked her up as arranged. As soon as Zella heard him beep the horn she ran out. She took his breath away as he watched her coming toward him, she looked beautiful in her pink and white dress. He opened the car door as he normally did for her and they set off to Hyde Park

Clive had packed up the Jaguar with a picnic hamper in a very extravagant but elegant picnic basket. He'd thought of everything: sandwiches, flask of tea, potato salad, coleslaw, fudge cake, even the blanket to sit on. They found a nice sunny spot in the park near the bandstand. Sighing contentedly with his head on Zella's lap, he stared up at her as she stroked his hair.

"You do know I like you, don't you?"

Zella nodded and smiled happily.

"Well… it's more. I love you… I love you, I hmmm I… I… *I want to marry you.*"

She laughed. "You're not good at this are you?"

"No… I've never asked anyone to marry me before."

"Oh is that what you're doing?" She giggled.

"Yes… you're laughing at me." He sat up and frowned.

"Yes… you're funny."

"I'm serious…"

"I'm teasing…"

"How can you tease at a time like this? He smiled. "I'm handing my heart and soul to you here and you tease?"

"OK, serious face!" She teased a little more. "You have to ask my mum."

"Is that a Yes?"

With that he lay back and told her she could resume stroking his hair.

"It's a Yes and … is that how it's going to be?" She giggled.

He gazes back up at her and tells her now he's the one doing the teasing.

She lowered her head to kiss him. He pulled her down to him kissing her back tenderly. She was happy. At last, she was really happy.

Chapter 8

When Florence and Patsy arrived in London, Zella went to meet them and told them that Clive was taking them to dinner, Florence thought that was a lovely gesture but said that he really didn't need to do that.

"Clive wants to tell you something. Well, *ask* you something."

Patsy, being the loudmouth she was, blurted out, *"She's pregnant"*, nearly causing Florence to choke on a mouthful of Victoria Sandwich.

"Patsy!" Zella screamed, patting their mother on the back.

"You're not pregnant?"

"No…"

"Oh, what a relief." Florence spluttered.

Just at that moment Clive knocked on the door. Zella let him and introduced him to her mum and Pasty

"Sooooo, what is it then ?" Patsy badgered.

"You'll have to wait and see."

"Ohhhwa, come on Zel spill the beans

"Well, I want to ask your mum a rather important
  question." Clive said, looking lovingly at Zella

As for Patsy, she thought it was all so boring. She put her
fingers in her mouth,

"*Ugh...barf!*" She said, and rolled her eyes.

"Shut up, Patsy, and don't be so vulgar." Florence
  scolded.

"This will be you one day."

"Only if it's with Alden."

Now there was a name that Zella hadn't heard for a while
and she tried to change the subject.

"He's like Alvin Preston, so dreamy."

"Are you stilling drooling over him?" Florence asked.

"Yes... I will marry him... you wait and see."

"Alden...?" Clive asked curiously.

"Alden is my boyfriend."

"Oh, I see."

Florence looked sternly across at Patsy. She had only met
Alden the once and hadn't realised that Patsy had seen him
more often. Patsy had jumped the gun yet again by
referring to him as her boyfriend. She knew there was a
lady in his life but still she dreamt of the day when he took
her in his arms and told her that he loved her.

That evening Clive picked them up and took them to a
fancy restaurant. Florence warned Patsy to be on her best
behaviour. She rolled her eyes and sighed.

"I'm not a child, Mother."

"Well, bear in mind you don't act like one then."

They made small talk over dinner and got to know each other a little more.

"This is nice, Clive. Thank you so much."

"I'm pleased you have enjoyed it, Mrs Russell. There is something I would like to ask you, if I may."

"Oh and what's that, my dear?"

"I would very much like to ask if I could have your daughter's hand in marriage."

Clive had quite won Florence over. She liked him and thought he would make Zella a very good husband.

"If Zella is happy then you have my blessing."

He looked across at Zella and smiled. She smiled lovingly back at him and nodded to him. The day after he took her to buy her engagement ring. He told her she could pick any ring she wanted so she looked around. In the end, she kept going back to the same ring, a beautiful, cushion-cut diamond halo with baguette stones.

"You like that one, don't you?"

"Yes… but…"

"But what…? I said *any* and I meant it."

"Really?"

"Yes."

She held her hand out admiring the ring. The sales assistant told her it looked so elegant on her as if it had been specially made for her.

"Yes, this is the one." She smiled.

"Excellent choice, Madam."

When Patsy and her mum saw the ring they just stared open-mouthed.

"Ohhhh… Zell" Patsy said, wide eyed.

"Darling… it's beautiful." Florence said, taking her hand
for a closer look.

Clive had made reservations at the Ritzy Pearl and he
invited his family along to meet Florence and Patsy. His
parents, , Violet and Edward, got on with them like a house
on fire. They talked about the wedding and how pleased
they were to have Zella as their daughter in law. Clive's
older brother, Harry, was there with his wife, Girt, and
their children, Sadie and Joseph. Harry ran the other branch
of Sapphire's in Newcastle. Florence told them about Zella
and Patsy's dad, how he had died in the war when he was
a young officer leaving her with two young babies.

"Hard times." Edward murmured.

Florence nodded in agreement before Violet suggested that
Edward took Florence and Patsy round Sapphire's before
they went home, making Patsy jump for joy. Once there,
she could scarcely believe her eyes. She did, however go
home with two of the very latest designs, *Zella Russell*
designs, in fact.

After Florence and Patsy left for home, it was back to work
for Zella. She had some new designs for Carlos *and* a
wedding to organise. Where to have it, well that was
another thing to think about. After all, she was only doing
it once.

Chapter 9

Chesterfield

Back home, Patsy had gone on a date with Arnold from the fishmongers in an attempt to get Alden's attention. She had insisted on going to the cinema as she knew Alden would be there, she'd heard him mention it to one of his friends, Arnold had always like Patsy. He'd asked her several times to go out with him, so you can imagine his joy when she finally said yes. He was very eager, in fact a little too eager. He kept trying to kiss her and she kept pushing him away but he didn't want to stop. When he became a little too forceful, she stood up and slapped him across the face. Alden noticed her and went over.

"Are you alright?"

"No..."

Alden turned to Arnold and told him sling his hook.

"Fuck off, Alden!"

"Leave her alone."

"Orrrr... what?"

76

"That is not how you treat a lady."

Arnold got up from his seat and told her she was nothing but a prick teaser, all this while the film was on. People were shouting at them to sit down or take it outside. Arnold stormed out. Alden suggested Patsy came to sit with him, then, after the film, they went to get some fish and chips. Patsy asked just for chips.

"No fish?"

"No thank you. I don't like fish."

"Have you ever tried it?"

"No…"

"Here, try this…" he held a piece of fish out to her.

"Hmm, this is good." as she took a bite.

"See…"

"Hmmm"

Patsy knew all along she liked fish, she jut wanted to find out if he would offer her any, it was all in the planning. They strolled along the street eating their supper.

"Are you in love with me yet?"

Alden laughed, "You really are so funny."

Pasty, however, was serious. Why would he think she was kidding? She'd never had to work this hard before. She loved him and she wanted him to love her back. She knew he had been involved with someone and he'd loved her but he was never with this mystery women. She had to be married, why else was she such a secret? It was the only reason Patsy could think of.

"Here we are, home safely."

"Thank you Alden… you were my hero tonight.

"Why do you over-dramatise everything?"

"Good night, Alden." Then she kissed him on the cheek

"Good night, Patsy."

Patsy watched him walk up the road, her heart beating so fast she could hardly breathe. He was the most handsome man she had ever seen, Black Rockabilly hair style, big grey eyes, high cheekbones and those kissable lips of his, she had dreamt about kissing those lips a thousand times.

Florence was waiting up for her when Patsy sauntered in as if she was on a cloud smiling to herself.

"Have you had a pleasant evening, my dear?"

"Oohh yes, mother. I had the best time."

"Arnold is a nice young man."

"He was not!" She said sharply.

"What do you mean, Patsy?"

"If it hadn't have been for Alden I would have had a problem. Alden rescued me."

Florence was more than a little concerned and demanded to know what Arnold had done; Patsy informed her mother that Arnold was not the gentleman that she thought he was.

"Oh my word, Patsy... Thank heavens for Alden."

"Yes... Alden was the perfect gentleman."

"You really like Alden, don't you?"

"Yes mum. I'm going to marry him, he just doesn't know it yet."

"Patsy, you can't *make* him love you, darling."

Patsy informed her mum that he *would* love her.

Unfortunately, Florence remembered the look on Zella's

face when he first turned up at their house. She felt there was more to that look than met the eye and she did wonder what happen to the young man Zella wanted to introduce to her. What a rush Zella had been in when she wanted to move to Stoke. Yes, there was more to this story that met the eye.

Next morning Patsy was up early and greeted Florence with a warm, loving kiss.

"Good morning, darling, you're very happy this morning."

"Yes… I'm happy, mum."

"I can see that."

Patsy ate her boiled eggs and set off to work. On the way Derick spotted her and shouted, she even stopped to talk to him. She normally ignored him or only wanted to talk about Alden, but this morning he did manage to get a full conversation out of her. It crossed his mind that she might be ill or coming down with something and he chuckled to himself. He thought he was funny even if no one else did.

Chapter 10

Alden had thought about going back to Stoke to look for Zella again but he didn't know where to start. He certainly couldn't ask Patsy but couldn't think of anyone else. Then, out of the blue, his boss shouted him into the office.

"Al… got a story for you, so pack a bag."

"Where, Boss?"

"Stoke."

"Stoke?" And he began to grin like a Cheshire cat.

"Well my, my… I have made someone happy today."

"Yes, Boss."

"What's in Stoke that's made you smile like that?"

"My best girl."

"Get gone…" he said, shaking his head, smiling, then shouted, "You're there to work, Alden."

Alden turned with his thumbs up, "Yes, Boss!"

He covered his story about new fashion in Stoke, all the while keeping an eye out for Zella. It was like looking in for a needle in a haystack, he was so disappointed yet again when he didn't find her.

As he settled back on the bus back to go back home, he casually glanced out of the window when he suddenly thought he spotted Zella. He stood up to get off the bus when a young man walked up to her and began hugging and kissing her. Alden was devastated. Unfortunately for him, he'd got the wrong end of the stick, not least was the fact it hadn't even been Zella. When he arrived back in Chesterfield he called in the boutique where she once had worked

"Hello Peggy."

"Can I help you?"

"You don't remember me?"

"Hmmm…" She studies his face a little while. "Alden isn't it? You're that reporter?"

"Yes… I was wondering if you have Zella's address in Stoke."

"No."

"Would you tell me if you did?"

"No, I wouldn't… Whatever you did, you broke that girl's heart, I haven't heard from her."

"It was a very big misunderstanding."

"I'm sorry."

Alden walked out in the street feeling utterly defeated. Yet again, he had lost the one girl he truly loved. He wasn't really in the mood that evening to meet up with his friends in the social club, but Derick badgered him so much he gave in.

"We're going to the bowling alley, coming?"

81

"Yep... why not"

They all ploughed in to the bowling alley and got two lanes to play. They were well into their second game when Mary noticed them.

"Don't look now, but your dream man is over there."

Patsy's eyes began to shine. "I'm going over."

"Patsy you should try to play a *little* hard to get."

"Why...? I know what I want and I want him."

"You should let him come to you."

"That's never gonna happen, is it?"

"Well, that should tell you something, then."

"Don't give me that."

Mary rolled her eyes and mumbled, "Well..."

"Shhhhh... Mary."

Patsy straightened herself up, checked her hair and makeup then adjusted her best assets before making her way over to Alden. Derick nudged him so he turned and spotted Patsy. He frowned, he really wasn't in the mood for her.

"Patsy?"

"Magnet, Hello, I mean *Alden*. I must stop calling you that."

"Patsy... How are you?"

"I'm really good."

"I'm so pleased for you, now what can I do for you?"

"What can you do for me? Nothing. I just came over to say hello."

"And now you have."

Patsy didn't like the way he had spoken to her, "You are so rude."

"But yet you still came over."

"UGH... where's that girlfriend you're supposed to have then?"

"None of your business."

Why did he keep blowing hot and cold? It was confusing not to mention it was driving her nuts. She was so infuriated, she stormed off, slipping along the way, to her embarrassment. She quickly regained her balance and headed back to Mary with her tail between her legs.

"That was a bit harsh, Al. She really likes you."

"It's not happening."

"Why?"

"Not interested. She'll get the message eventually."

"You wouldn't mind me asking her out then?"

"No... be my guest."

Derick went over to Patsy and asked her she if would like to go to the dance the following week. Still angry with Alden, she immediately accepted Derick's invitation, telling him she would love to go with him.

"Great! I'll pick you up at seven then?"

"I'll be ready."

"I need your address..."

She giggled. "Oops, yes of course

She wrote her address on the back of his hand and told him not to lose it, then giggled again. He laughed too, saying he hoped he didn't lose it and told her that she had one hell of a sense of humour.

Peggy looked thoughtful as she sat down in front of the coal fire with her pot of tea and a slice of Madeira cake and began to write her letter to Zella. She did wonder what Alden had done so wrong that Zella didn't want to see him anymore. She knew Zella so well, it had to have been something very bad for her to cut him off so suddenly because she was such a warm, loving young lady.

Dearest Zella

I hope all is well, hope are enjoying your adventure in London, you have got some exciting times ahead of you I'm sure of that. You must tell me all your news so hurry and write back to me.

Oh and Alden came in the boutique today. He was asking if I had your address for Stoke but I told him I hadn't heard from you. He looks so sad, Zell.

Hope to hear from you soon

love Peg xxx

A couple of weeks later Peggy received a letter in reply. Peggy was excited, when she saw Zella's hand writing on the envelope, she rushed to open it. She was eager to read Zella news, which she read as she made bubble and squeak from the previous night's leftovers. As she was buttering some bread, she stopped half way through as she saw that Zella had was talking about marriage.

My dear Peggy

I have some news you may want to hear. I'm getting married, I have met a lovely man, his name is Clive, I will be Mrs Berry. Can you believe I'm getting married? He owns the super store Sapphires. My career is going well too. I'm head of design's at Carlos Nomikos' biggest Factory, isn't that exciting, Peggy?

Lots and lots of love, Zell xx

Peggy was a hopeless romantic. She had lost the man she was going to marry in the war, she had never got over losing the love of her life, nor did she think she ever would. They had been sweethearts for many years and planned to get married when he came back from fighting for his country but, sadly, he never made it back home.

She hoped that Zella would be happy, she just wanted the best for her as she thought a lot about her. She was so much more than just an ex-employee, she was her friend and besides she loved a happy ending. She brewed a pot of tea whilst she read the rest of Zella's news but not once did she mention Alden's name.

Chapter 11

Dance night at the *Green Moon*

Patsy had worked all week and was ready for the weekend. She was really looking forward to the dance even though it wasn't Alden taking her. Derick was a nice young man, tall with greased-back mousey brown hair, polite, considerate and well mannered, he came to the door to pick her up and introduced himself to Florence. She liked him immediately and he got full approval. She did wonder what had happened with Alden. Florence couldn't keep up with Patsy's young men although she felt there were far too many and hoped she was a lady when she was out.

Patsy and Derick arrived at the *Green Moon* dance hall. Patsy looked around but there was no sign of Alden anywhere. He must be with his married woman.

"Do you know who Alden's Girlfriend is, Derick?"

"No… never seen her. Heard a lot about her, though."

"What's her name?"

"I don't know that either, I don't know much about her. I know he loves her."

"I think she's married."

"Married?"

"Why else wouldn't we have seen her?"

"Hmmm… fair point… but I don't think she's married."

"She must be. What other explanation would there be for not being out in public with her"

Derick stood for a moment in thought about Patsy's suggestion. It was fair to say she had a point and why wouldn't he have introduced her to his best friend or told him her name if he had nothing to hide.

A short while later, Alden walked in with a very attractive young lady. She looked so refined, blonde with a brushed under bob, wearing little makeup but luscious red lips. This must be the woman he was seeing, the green-eyed monster reared its big ugly head, Patsy was so jealous.

Derick stood with his mouth open as they walked past. Patsy pushed her finger to Derick's chin, closing his mouth.

"You're catching flies, Derick."

"And you're *jealous.*"

"I'm not!"

Patsy watched Alden with this woman all night. Every time she looked over at him, this beautiful blonde was draped all over him, kissing him, not quite as refined as Patsy had first thought. Derick, however, was getting annoyed.

"I thought you were with me?"

"I am…"

"So why are you watching Alden and his lady friend?"

"I'm not. He can do whatever he wants, I'm not bothered."

"Patsy I like you, but can I give you some advice? Forget him."

"Ugh… Why do you feel the need to tell me what I should do?"

"You're wasting your time. You are going to get hurt."

"I won't !

Derick really liked Patsy. He knew she was jealous and he wasn't going to play second fiddle to anyone, not even his best pal Alden. He dropped Patsy home after the dance and decided to forget about her. It was only a week later that he met Bessie who was destined to be the love of his life.

Meanwhile Zella was mixing with new sets of people, people who could help her career. She had met some designers from Paris and Italy and she wanted to know everything there was to know.

Other designers had started to notice Zella Russell and she liked it. Clive knew a lot of people and introduced her to many of them. Zella was ambitious, hardworking and dedicated. Carlos loved working alongside her, they made a great team. He could tell Zella was destined to do great things, her talent was going to take her all the way to the top.

Chapter 12

The Wedding, 1957

Patsy hadn't seen Alden for weeks. He'd been away covering stories in different cities and she'd wondered if he was with that women. She was still feeling quite jealous just thinking about it. Anyway, she had to pick a dress for Zella's wedding, come Saturday. She and Florence had decided to go to the new store that was opening that day in town. They wandered in and were browsing the dresses when Patsy spotted Alden and rushed over.

"Hello, stranger. Where have you been?"

"Hello, what are you doing here?"

"Looking for a new dress."

"Oh I see… special occasion?"

"Zella's wedding."

"Zella is getting married?"

Alden's heart sank and he felt sick to the pit of his stomach. He couldn't believe Zella was about to get married.

"I've just had a good idea! Why don't you come with us?"

"No, Patsy…"

"Why?"

"Honestly, I couldn't think of anything worse."

"Alden… you are so rude at times."

"Sorry… but Zella wouldn't want me there."

"Why would you think that?"

"She doesn't like me."

"What makes you say that?"

"Trust me she doesn't like me, besides I'm going to see *the Shedrons* with a guy from the office who'd got free tickets as he was covering a story."

Patsy told him he was lucky.

She would love to see them, they were one of her favourite bands, particularly their song, *'Come back baby'*.

"Well, enjoy the wedding."

"I will…but I'd rather be going to see *the Shedrons*."

Alden walked away with his head hung low in defeat. He was devastated, he had lost Zella to another man. He still loved her with all his heart, there really was no other women for him. This news was going spoil his whole weekend

❧ ❧

Come the Thursday, Florence and Patsy caught the train for Zella's wedding. It wasn't going to be a big flash wedding, just Clive's parents, his brother, his brother's wife and their children, Zella's mum, Patsy, Carlos and Miriam and a handful of friends at the register office.

She hadn't bought a big flash wedding dress either. She had picked a stained oyster sliver strapless tulle layer dress with a crystal waist band and bolero jacket. Not to be outdone, Clive had got himself a Marlon James suit, a classic.

After the wedding they went back to Clive's mum and dads for a wedding tea of Chicken and tarragon, cream cheese, walnut and watercress sandwiches with a stand of coffee and walnut, lemon and cherry cakes, all washed down with fresh elderflower, apple and ginger cocktails or something stronger if that was your preference, not forgetting a good old pot of tea. Florence had made their wedding cake, a small two tier cake with an iced heart and in the middle stood a bride and groom.

After the tea, Zella and Clive set off on their honeymoon. They spent a couple of days in a small bed and breakfast in a lovely thatched cottage in Cornwall, taking long walks on the beach and browsing round the shops. Zella wanted to see what the ladies were wearing, she wanted to see if she could get some inspiration.

The lady that owned the cottage made a really nice meat and potato pie and her Victoria sandwich was to die for, Zella told her she must have gone up a size with all the wonderful food she had eaten for the past few days and they surely wanted to come back, maybe on their anniversary.

Meanwhile Carlos was at Fashion event, Ruth Johnson was showing her collection alongside Dorian Fabron and Ingrid Halvorson, when a model strutted down the cat walk in a beautiful champagne coloured dress. Carlos thought he recognised the design, but where on earth had he seen it?

The next day was Zella's first day back after her honeymoon and she headed to Carlos's office there she found him on the floor with all her designs scattered everywhere.

"Carlos, what on earth are you doing?"

"I'm looking for something but I don't know if my hunch is right. Oh yes, I hope you had a wonderful honeymoon..."

"I had lovely time... Carlos, please explain – what you are looking for?"

"Zella, look at all your designs"

Puzzled, Zella looked down and asked him why. He told her he had a bad feeling and she asked him what it was about.

"Look carefully Zella... are they all there?"

"Yes... I think so"

"Are you absolutely sure"

She looks again, closer this time and realises there is one missing.

"I knew it... Is it the Champagne Trumpet Tully?"

"Yes, but how did you know?"

"Do you remember Ruth Johnson coming in to see me?"

"Yes... I need to come up with something better – I remember she wasn't keen on them."

"Ohhhhh...yes... she was!

Carlos told Zella how he had seen this dress on a model at the event he was at which meant that Ruth had stolen the design. Zella was shocked to say the least. Carlos told her people loved this dress, the number of ladies ordering this dress was amazing, but he knew he had seen this design and he knew that Zella had shown it to him.

"But she …"

"Yes, I know."

"But how did she get the design?"

"I made the mistake of leaving her alone in my office."

Zella was totally stunned that a well-known designer like Ruth needed to steal from an unknown. Carlos wanted to take it to the press, but Zella pointed out how unlikely it was the could prove that it wasn't her design. Carlos was so angry, and so apologetic to Zella for his clumsiness and stupidity.

She assured him it one of those things and she forgave him, after all he had helped her by giving her a job she loved. He told he would not be making the same mistake again and he would be paying Ruth a visit.

He did, too, the following day. He barged passed the receptionist and faced Ruth.

"How could you?"

"What are you talking about, Carlos?"

"The Champagne Trumpet Tully design, you stole that design from Zella."

"Prove… it…" She said cockily.

"You know I can't… and furthermore, you know Zella can't either."

"It's dog eat dog in this business, darling, and you know it!"

Carlos's anger was boiling over. Giving her a withering look he shook his head in disbelief .

"I thought we were friends, obviously not."

"Ohhhh come on, darling."

Carlos turned his back on her and left, slamming the door behind him.

        ❧   ❧

Alden was having a good day and he was about have an even better evening. At the dance where *the Shedrons* were playing, he met the group and interviewed them back stage. Derick smiled at Bessie and pointed out a row of young ladies all vying for his attention, all of them sat on the sidelines, waiting and hoping he would ask one of them to dance. He shook his head.

"How do you do it?"

"Do what?"

"Look at them all, swooning over you."

Alden just shrugged his shoulders. "I dunno."

"It's everywhere we go."

"Lucky I guess."

"I reckon it's 'cause you look like Alvin Preston." Bessie jumped in.

"No I don't … I wish I did"

"You do have a look of him."

"Well, in that case, I'd better use it to my advantage."

He sauntered over to a very attractive brunette and asked her to dance and as they made their way to the dance floor, he complimented her on her dress.

"Oh Thank you… it's a Zella Russell design."

"Did you say Zella Russell?"

"Yes… why?"

"Well, you know where that dress would look really good?"

"No…"

"Draped over the end of my bed."

She giggled. "You are bad."

"Yeah… and you like it."

At the end of the evening Alden left with Dora. They went back to his bed and breakfast and crept to his room. They sat on the bed kissing passionately. His hand moved up her leg, finally reaching her stocking top when she stopped him.

"You won't tell anyone will you?"

"No… don't worry."

Pulling her panties down, he moved between her thighs. Pulling himself out of his trousers he quickly pushed himself into her, moving back and forth. She groaned with pleasure. As his rhythm got a little faster, she pulled him closer and moaned, louder and louder until he had to put his hand to her mouth to muffle her groans. When he released her they lay there puffing and panting. Suddenly there was a bang on the door

"Mr Pearce?"

"Yes…"

"I hope you haven't got a young lady in there!"

"No…" as he puts his finger to Dora's lips. "shhhhh…"

Dora was trying desperately not to giggle. They waited a little while then Alden walked her home. She asked if she would see him again and he told he was going back home in the morning so it was very unlikely, he was honest if nothing else.

The next morning Alden, Derick and Bessie came down for their breakfast then went to get the bus back to Chesterfield.

"Where did you get to last night?"

"Here…"

"With that bird…?"

"A gentleman never tells."

"Yes… but you're not one."

Alden laughed. "Yeah… I am."

"It was you that the landlord was shouting at too… wasn't it?"

Alden grinned, winking smugly.

"Hmmm boys, the bus is here." Bessie shouted.

When the bus came they jumped on and settled down for the journey back Alden fell straight asleep, he'd had rather an exhausting night before. Soon they were back in Chesterfield. They didn't have time to go home and freshen up, instead they got off the bus and headed straight in to work.

Bessie was heading home and told Derick she would see him later, planting a long kiss on his lips. Alden grabbed his jacket and dragged him away from her.

"Those lips will still be there later – our jobs may not be, come on!"

"Bye… boys."

"Bye Bessie!" They shouted in unison as they ran down the street.

"Derick, you're late!" A voice shouted as he sauntered in

"Sorry Boss… bus was…"

Stan interrupted him, telling him he didn't want to hear it and he better make up the time. Derick nodded and went and sat at his desk .

"Alden, I want you to chase this up."

"On it, Stan."

Alden looked down at the piece of paper Stan had given him and asked if he could take Derick with him. Stan asked for what reason, it was only going to take one reporter to cover the story. Alden pointed out that Derick was a better cameraman than him. Stan ummed and arred for a few seconds then agreed.

"I want this story, Alden!"

"You got it Stan…." He shouted at Derick to grab his camera.

"What we covering?"

"Kitty Laine… She's appearing at *the Green Moon* dance hall, for one night only, so get your stuff together and get some great picture otherwise Stan will lose his marbles."

Derick was excited but he knew he had to get the best pictures of Kitty Laine. As they approached the Green Moon there she was, posing for pictures. Derick's heart skipped a beat, she looked so good and so young – certainly younger than her nineteen years. What Alden and Derick didn't know was they had another surprise in store when Cissy Grant walked out and stood next to Kitty. Cissy had just finished her first musical in Hollywood, she was just twenty and, boy could that lady dance. Hollywood was going crazy over her. Alden asked a few questions and Derick took some fabulous pictures and they even got to chat to Kitty and Cissy.

"Thanks Al…."

"I knew you would want to cover this, I just hope you got some good photos."

Chapter 13

1958

The following weekend Pasty went to the Brocksy Mecca with her friends for the rock 'n' roll night. Alden caught Patsy's eyes from across the room and beckoned her over to him. He'd had a few drinks and was a little drunk.

"Hello, Alden,"

"Where have you been?"

"I told you… I went to Zella's wedding."

"Oh… yeah."

"I've come to ask you to dance."

"You come to ask me to dance… I thought it was supposed to be the other way round."

"If I left it to you, you'd never ask."

Alden laughed and shook his head. "Come on then."

They did a few jives then a slow one came on. Patsy thought that Alden wouldn't dance a slow one with her and she turned to make her way back to her friends.

Alden grabbed her hand and pulled her to him, putting his hand tight round her waist. He started to sway with her, getting closer and closer, his hands getting tighter. She was in heaven and looked helplessly into his eyes.

"I love you."

"You love me?"

"Yes. I would do anything for you, Alden."

"That's interesting."

"Are you still seeing that woman?"

"Enough talk."

He leant in to kiss her and of course she kissed him back, this is what she'd had been waiting for.

On the sideline, Derick saw Alden with Patsy. He felt a little jealous, he always seemed to be drawn back to Patsy even though he was happy with Bessie.

"Let's go"

"Where are we going Alden?"

"For a walk, so we can be alone"

They walked along the High Street hand in hand then they took a short cut down the gully. Alden stopped and took her in his arms, kissing her passionately, she had finally got what she wanted. She kissed him back and the kiss became deeper and more intense. Alden's hand started to wander, he started lifting her skirt up. His hand got higher and higher until he reached her stocking tops. He moved his hand between her thighs and began to pleasure her with his fingers. She moaned as he took it to the next level. Pulling her panties to the side, he pushed himself into her, moving himself back and forth as she moaned with delight. Finally, he collapsed against her as he released.

"Ohhhhh yessss, Ahhhhhh!" She ran her fingers through his hair. "I love you, Alden."

"No, you don't."

"Yes I do!"

"You wouldn't love me if you knew."

"Knew what?"

"It doesn't matter."

He pushed his manhood back in his trousers and straightened himself-up.

He told her he would take her home. She pulled her dress down and asked him again what he meant.

"Nothing...Come on I'll take you home."

"Alden, what did you mean?"

"Forget it..."

This must be the married women he was talking about, Patsy thought to herself as he walked her home.

"Good night, Patsy."

"Alden?"

He walked back over to her and kissed her forehead softly.

"Good night."

She stood and watched him walk away. What had just happened? Where did this leave her? She wondered what would happen next. Was he going to dump his married women and be with her? After all, she had just given herself to him. She was a little confused at this point but she needed to know.

She thought she would ask him the next day but Alden had been assigned to cover a story in Bradford and was away for a couple of weeks. When he got back, Stan told him not to get too comfy at his desk as he had another assignment for him.

"Where…?"

"London."

"London…?" Alden's eyes lit up.

"Oh, I see you like that."

"Yes… Yes I do."

"Well, you are interviewing Sapphires' Owner, Clive Berry."

"Clive Berry?" He remembered Clive from the races.

As the train pulled in Euston Station, he walked to the bus stop and caught the bus to Camden Town. After he had booked himself in to a bed and breakfast near the store, he got his things together and made his way to Sapphires. Clive was there to greet him .

"Hello… Mr Berry…?"

"Yes… You are Mr Pearce, I presume?"

"Yes… You don't remember me, do you?"

Clive paused momentarily. "Alden?"

"Yeah."

"It's really good to see you."

"Yeah, good to see you… now, that tour of Sapphires"

"Yeah, of course."

As he walked Alden round the store Clive made small talk, asking him how he'd been and asking about Derick. Alden took the shots he need to cover his story, interviewing him while they walked.

"The store was opened by your father's father, wasn't it?"

"Yes… In 1930. It was just a small shop then, my father made it into what it is today."

"But you've branched out with a few other stores in different parts of the country, haven't you?"

"Yes. I have bought three shops; you *have* done your homework."

"I like to have all my facts. Well, it's been a pleasure, Mr Berry. Thank you."

"My pleasure… How long are you in London?"

"Just a couple of days."

"Well, maybe you would like to come to our event tomorrow, it might give you some more to write in your article."

Yes…that would be great. Thanks."

When Alden arrived at Sapphires the next evening, it seemed to be quite a big event. Clive explained that his wife had come up with the idea for a fashion show in the store. They had never done anything like this before so it was a bit of a trial. Clive tapped Zella on the shoulder.

"I would like you to meet our reporter this evening."

Zella literally froze to the spot when she turned and came face to face with Alden. Alden was also in shock. He hadn't realised that Clive was the man Zella had married. Patsy had never told him. Mind you, he never really gave her the chance to.

"Zella…?"

"Alden…"

"Do you know each other?" Clive asked

Zella quickly interrupted, "Yes, Alden is a friend of my sister's."

Alden looked straight at her. "I think I'm a little more than that."

"I thought that name rang a bell, aren't you Patsy's beau?" Clive asked inquisitively.

Alden was just about to say 'no' when Zella cut him off, telling Clive his dad was trying to get his attention. Clive said he would be right back, giving Zella time to tell Alden to go.

"I have to talk to you."

"Get back under that stone you came from and leave me alone"

"Zella, please talk to me."

"No… What are you doing here?"

"Covering a story"

"You have to leave."

"I'm working…this is my job."

"Ugh… you took this story on purpose."

"How was I supposed to know you were his wife?"

He told her he needed to see her and asked her to meet him at Camden. She told him not to bother; she had nothing to say to him. He told her if she didn't meet him next day, he would make a scene.

"Oh, OK…"

"Thank you…"

Clive was making his way back over to them. Zella didn't want Clive to know about Alden, all she had told him about her previous relationship was that it hadn't worked out. She had never even mentioned Alden's name.

After seeing Alden that evening, she couldn't help but think about their time together. She had loved him so much. She still couldn't get her head round how he could have done that to her. It didn't add up, it really didn't make sense. She couldn't sleep for thinking about it, it just wasn't him.

She got out of bed and went to sit downstairs otherwise she was going to wake Clive up with all her tossing and turning. She was deep in thought when Clive called out to her, making her lose her chain of thought.

"Zella, what are you doing down there?"

"I couldn't sleep."

"Why are you in the dark?"

"I didn't want to wake you by putting lights on."

"What's wrong?"

He took her hand gently, pulling her up from the chair. He put his arms around her, drawing her closer and leaning in to kiss her softly.

"Come on, let's go back to bed."

He cuddled into her, gently kissing her neck. Lowering his hand, he pulled her nightdress up, his kisses becoming deeper and more intense as he slipped his pyjama bottoms down. Before she knew it, he had moved between her thighs, pressing himself down in to her slowly, moving back and forth in steady rhythm. He was breathing heavily, his steady stokes became faster and faster until he groaned as he climaxed. Still panting, he rolled off her before turning over and falling asleep. She lay there feeling a little deflated, wide awake and staring at the ceiling. Alden kept coming back into her thoughts. She didn't need this feeling, she didn't *want* this feeling.

Next day, she made her way to Camden, all the while going over in her head what she was going to say to him. When Alden saw her walking towards him he was so relieved – finally he could tell her what had really happened and how Patsy had got the wrong end of the stick. Zella wasn't there to listen, though, no sooner had she approached him than she told him to go home and never to come near her ever again.

"Zella, you need to listen to me."

"No... I don't."

"Yes, you do!" He said, grabbing her hand.

"Let go!

"But I love you…"

"I don't love you."

Alden let go of her hand and let his head drop.

"I see…" Her last statement had cut like a knife.

"Just leave me alone, I love my husband and you are a bad memory."

Alden looked down at his feet, told she shouldn't worry he would never bother her again then walked away. Zella watched him walk down the street, knowing she had hurt him. She had lashed out, not something she was proud of but nevertheless it was done now.

She looked so tired when she arrived in work that Carlos thought she was ill and told her to go home.

"No, I'm fine, Carlos."

"You don't look well, Sweetheart."

"I just didn't sleep very well, that's all."

"Have you something bothering you?"

Zella didn't really want to go in to it so she told him there was nothing, it was probably only about thinking about designs and coming up with something new and exciting. He liked the sound of that but told her not to lose sleep over it.

"Go home, get some rest."

"Thank you, Carlos."

She kissed him gently on the cheek. Although she was so tired, she knew that working would keep her from thinking about Alden

Alden was sat back on his seat in the train going over what she had said. He'd been so shocked at her statement, it had hurt him to the bone. He simply didn't believe it, she must be *lying*.

Chapter 14

Alden returned home feeling as if things simply couldn't get any worse. Unfortunately, he was mistaken. As he walked along the high street he suddenly bumped into Patsy. She was really pleased to see him and he asked her if she wanted to go for a cup of tea.

"I wanted to talk to you about the other week. You know that what happened was a…"

She knew what he was going to say. She interrupted him by blurting out that she was pregnant.

"What…?" He thought he'd heard that wrong, he *hoped* he'd heard that wrong.

"I'm pregnant." She sobbed.

"Are you sure?"

"I have missed my period."

"That doesn't mean you're pregnant."

"I'm never late, I never miss."

"Shit…What I mean is… Oh, I don't know what I mean."

"My mum is going to kill me." Tears rolled down her face faster and faster.

"Don't worry." He bit his lip.

"What am I going to do?"

"Hmm…"

"Alden, *what am I going to do?*"

Alden didn't want to marry Patsy, or anyone else for that matter if he couldn't have the woman he wanted. Marriage wasn't on his agenda, but he did know the honourable thing to do.

"Don't worry, Patsy,we'll get married, they never need to know."

"Oh, Alden!" She said, flinging her arms round him and kissing him.

The next day, Alden went to Patsy's to ask her if he could have Patsy's hand in marriage. Florence looked oddly at Alden and questioned their relationship. It seemed strange to her to want to be married when she thought that they were no longer seeing each other.

"I didn't realise you were still seeing each other, let alone *that* serious."

"Yes… I love your daughter, Mrs Russell."

Technically, of course, he was telling the truth. He *did* love her daughter, just not the one he was asking to marry. Florence smiled and agreed to the marriage and asked when they were planning the wedding. He told her he wanted to marry Patsy straight away.

"Why the rush…?"

"I will be away on assignments soon and I would like to be married before I go."

Florence was more than a little suspicious at this. Maybe she shouldn't ask, she had given her approval but she had the idea that there were some little feet about to appear. She called Zella to let her know her sister was getting married and Zella asked who the lucky man was.

"Alden…"

"Alden?…. Hmmm, Great –she said she would marry him"

"Yes she did, didn't she?" Florence was all round suspicious, she heard the hurt in Zella's voice as she thought Patsy was in the family way.

"When…?"

"Before he goes away, in a few weeks apparently, a tad suspicious."

"Ohhhh… Mother."

Zella put the phone down and sighed, her eyes filling up. Small pearl drops began to run down her face. She knew she had to put all this behind her once and for all, she would have to have him in her life now as he was going to be her brother in law. She only wanted her sister to be happy so she just had to get on with it. Even so, her mother was right, it *was* awfully suspicious. But at the end of the day it was what Patsy wanted. She said she would marry her dream man, even though it would break her sister's heart, but she wasn't to know that. That was a secret that had to stay a secret forever.

Patsy was so excited. She and Mary had gone shopping. Mary wanted to how she had got Alden to change his mind. Winking at Mary, she told her, "I have my ways, Mary."

"Really…? What ways?"

"Why, my natural charm, of course!"

"What happened to the love of his life then?"

"Mary... Why do you want to spoil this for me?" She snapped.

"I don't..."

"It seems that way. You're my best friend, you should be happy for me."

"I am... but, well, he wasn't interested not so long ago and then there was his mystery woman. I'm just trying to understand."

"Ohhhh, Mary, just be happy for me."

At the office, Alden's friends threw him a party. Mary wasn't the only one with questions, Derick was as confused as she was.

"What happened, Al?"

"What...?"

"Why the sudden change of heart?"

"Things change, Derick.

"Not you, Al... What happened to the woman you couldn't live without, your mystery lady...you know... the one you are so secretive about, the one you couldn't even tell you best bud about?"

"Derick... let's leave it... OK?"

Derick wasn't completely sure what Alden was playing at, but none of it felt right. He knew Alden and this woman was not completely in the past by any means. He never remembered Alden telling any woman he loved them yet he had sworn undying love to this one. No, marrying Patsy wasn't like Alden at all.

Chapter15

A couple of day before the wedding Zella and Clive travelled over to Chesterfield. Zella had taken it for granted that she and Clive could stay with Florence but when they got there they found she'd already got a full house. Alden offered them a room at his place but Zella refused point blank.

"It's no bother"

"That's really generous of you Alden." Clive thanked him.

Zella said that Clive could easily get them a hotel.

"Yes, I'm easy. Whatever is the easiest."

"I wouldn't hear of it." Alden insisted

Pasty pulled Zella to one side, "Why don't you like Alden?"

"Pardon…?"

"You heard me, Zella."

"I have nothing against him."

"He told me you don't like him."

"I don't know where he has got that from"

"So… accept his invitation.

Zella sighed, reluctantly accepting. She really didn't want to do this, she didn't feel it was right. However, she didn't want to raise suspicion. That evening Alden took everyone for a meal, then afterwards they went to the *Green Moon* wherethey were playing Motown. Florence was going to go home but Zella insisted she stay for a while. When everyone got up to go to the dance floor, Florence took hold of Alden's hand and asked him to sit down.

"Does my daughter know you're in love with her?"

"I hope so, we *are* getting married tomorrow"

"I didn't mean Patsy… I meant Zella."

"I don't understand."

"Yes… I think you do. I've seen the way you look at Zella."

Alden looked at the floor, "Mrs Russell I can…"

Florence cut him off. "Don't come between my girls."

"I don't intend to."

As the evening drew to a close Alden, Zella and Clive headed back to the house. Alden showed Zella and Clive to their room then wished them good night.

"Good night Alden" Clive said then turned to Zella. "Do you not like Alden?"

"That the second time I've been asked that today… why does everyone keep asking me that?"

"It's the way you are with him."

"I hardly know him."

"I thought you did."

"Well let's just say he proved me wrong… Good night,
Clive."

Clive wondered what she meant about proving her wrong
it was an odd thing for her to say. Zella couldn't sleep, she
was tossing and turning for hours before she crept down
stairs and put a pan of milk on the stove. Suddenly she
heard footsteps, Alden had heard movement downstairs
and had come down to investigate. Popping his head round
the kitchen door he made Zella jump out of her wits

"I'm sorry, Zella."

"No I'm sorry – did I wake you?

"No."

"Why did you do that?"

"What?"

"Offer to put us up for the wedding… We could have
gone to a hotel."

"I…wanted…"

Cutting him off before he could say another word, she tells
him she was making some hot milk and asked if he would
like some.

"Yeah… why not?"

"Could you not sleep either …? Are you nervous?"

"No…"

"No…?"

"I was fine until I saw you again."

"Don't do that… I should not even be here in your
home… It's wrong."

"Zella… I love you."

"You love my sister?"

114

"No... I don't."

"Why are you marrying her, if you don't love her?"

"She's pregnant."

"She's *what*...? Does my mother know?"

Alden shook his head, moved his chair closer to Zella and took her hand.

"I love *you*"

She got up from the table.

"I don't want to hear this, you are marrying my sister tomorrow."

She moved over to the sink to rinse the empty mugs. Suddenly Alden was very close and, as she turned around, he stepped in and kissed her. She sighed heavily and, forgetting herself, kissed him back. He moved his hands round her waist and pulled her closer but she suddenly pulled away.

"No... No, Stop!" She pushed him back .

"Why?"

"You have to do right by my sister."

"I'll call it all off"

"No, you can't do that. She needs you... that baby needs you."

As she tried to move out of reach he took hold of her hand and pulled her back.

"Don't make me do this."

"You've got to."

"No, I don't."

"Yes you do."

What they couldn't know was that Clive was stood behind the door, listening to the whole conversation. He had heard everything. He had assumed that there was still something going on between them and he was very upset. Not knowing what to do, he crept back upstairs and pretended to be asleep.

Zella pulled away, leaving Alden standing there and made her way upstairs. She slipped into bed and lay there with tears rolling down her face, trying desperately try not to make a sound. Clive knew she was crying, he could feel her sobbing.

The next morning Alden had made some breakfast and was sat at the table with Clive. Clive was very frosty and stared at him. When Zella came down all Alden could do was watch Zella, practically begging her with his eyes. Clive could see how he looking at her and stood up, telling her he was going up to get dressed. He waited on the foot of stairs for a moment, leaving Zella at the table. Predictably, Alden grabbed her hand from across the table.

"Zella, please!"

"No don't. This never happened – you are marrying my sister and her happiness is all that matters to me." She whispered

"I told her."

"You told her what?"

"That I loved someone else"

"Shhhhh… Why did you do that?"

"Because I do. Why did you run away? Why did you never let me explain?"

"She… she told me she loves you."

At the wedding Clive decided to tell Zella what he had heard. Se tried to pretend she didn't know what he was talking about.

"I know.

"Know what?"

"About you and Alden... why you are like you are with him"

"There is no me and Alden."

"Zella... I heard you and him in the kitchen last night. I was on the stairs. Do you still love him, Zella?"

"NO..."

Zella didn't know what to say. She didn't want to talk about this today of all days, she didn't want to talk about it full stop. To put and end to it, she said she would explain everything when they got home. This was not the time or the place to discuss it, she explained, but it wasn't what it seemed. She calmed him down and convinced him to wait until they got home

"There is nothing between us."

"Really...?"

"Really, I will tell you everything later, I promise."

Patsy appeared in the doorway of the register office looking radiant in her lace full circle skirt wedding dress with full petticoat. Alden looked very dashing in his teddy boy drapes suit. As Patsy walked towards him Alden turned but instead of looking at his bride, he looked straight down at Zella. Zella put her head down, trying not to look at him. She was fighting back her emotions. She had to, for both their sakes.

They had a lovely reception with a smashing sit-down tea. Dainty sandwiches, honey and mustard sausages, pork pie, vegetable pie and mixture of cakes were all washed down with tea, raspberry lemonade and for the more adventurous a glass of wine. They had a small, two tier cake beautifully decorated with a heart shaped flower.

Derick had got a young pianist to play and some people started dancing. Alden muttered something about needing a proper drink and headed for the bar in the corner. He ordered himself a whiskey sour which he downed in one, then ordered another, Derick had noticed how stressed he was and went over to him.

"What are you doing over here?"

"I needed a fuckin' drink."

"Ain't the groom supposed to be happy?"

"Yeah… if he marries the woman he loves."

"What did you get married for then?"

"Keep it to yourself, she's pregnant."

Derick sighed and shook his head.

"She's *pregnant*? Yours I presume? When the fuck did that happen?"

That night at that fuckin' dance. I'd had too much to drink… I obviously thought it was a good idea at the time."

"That's shitty. I'm sorry… the other woman you were seeing, what happened to her?"

"Oh…. D… don't fuckin' ask."

"What a fucking mess Al, I'm glad it ain't Bessie up the duff! "

Unfortunately, Bessie had wandered over to see what Derick and Alden were talking about and when she overheard she blanched and turned around, tears welling in her eyes.

❧ ❧

Alden spotted Zella heading outside. She needed some air. Her heart was secretly breaking but she couldn't show it. She lit a cigarette and inhaled deeply, blowing a mist of smoke in the air. As the smoke cleared, there stood Alden.

"Talk to me, Zella."

"It's too late"

"It's never too late."

He looked into her eyes and caressed her cheek with the back of his fingers. He just wanted to take her in his arms and take all the pain away.

"Go back to your bride."

"I don't want to."

"You've got to.

He took her hand. "Zella..."

"Then I will go – we can't be out here together."

Zella headed toward the door she turned her head back. Alden mouthed 'I love you'. Clive was on his way out and bumped into her.

"Where have you been?"

"Having a cigarette…"

He told her he was heading to the gents but he was heading outside. He knew Alden was out there and wasn't going to mince his words.

"Stay away from my wife." He said aggressively.

"She's my sister in-law."

"I heard you last night. Stay away from her."

"I don't know what you mean."

"Ohhhh… Yes you do… Now I'm only going to say this one more time, stay the fuck away from my wife!"

Alden didn't like Clive's threats but he knew he couldn't retaliate. He simply went back inside to Patsy.

The next day, Patsy and Alden went for two nights away in Blackpool. Alden had booked them into a bed and breakfast for their honeymoon. The last time he had been in Blackpool it was the amazing day he'd had with Zella. As Alden hung his jacket up on the door, Patsy sat on the bed admiring her wedding ring.

"*Mrs Pearce* – I like that"

He moved over to her and kissed her forehead.

"I want more than that, Mr Pearce."

"What about the baby?"

"It'll be fine."

Little did Alden know that Patsy had found out she wasn't pregnant a week before their wedding. She had got the man she wanted and wasn't intending to lose him. She needed to get pregnant and soon.

She moved closer, leaning in to kiss him and he kissed her back. Every time he closed his eyes, Zella appeared in front of him. He tried desperately hard to put her at the back of his mind.

Trying to make the best of a bad situation, he leered at Patsy and started to undress her, sliding his fingers up her thighs. She responded eagerly as he slid between her thighs. Suddenly, he jumped up.

"What's wrong, Alden?"

"I'm sorry… I can't."

"Alden, it's OK… the baby will be fine, I promise. It's just nerves, that all… it happens."

"*What?*… There's nothing wrong with my dick. I can get hard, it's nothing to do with that"

He stomped out of the room to the bathroom and put his head against the cool mirror. Sighing heavily, he thought, '*I can't do this.*'

When he walked back into the bedroom he began to button his shirt up. Patsy wondered what he was doing.

"Alden…?"

"I'm going for a walk…I need to get some fresh air."

"*No!*" She wailed.

She demanded to know what was wrong he didn't touch her on their wedding night and now this.

"I just need to clear my head, Patsy. OK?"

Grabbing his coat he walked out leaving Pasty sat on the bed. She knew he was thinking about that woman. It struck her that she would never get pregnant if he kept doing this and he would find out she'd lied to him.

Meanwhile, Alden took along walk along the sea front. It was cold and the sea was wild, he stood watching it crash over the walls. He stood there for hours. He didn't want to go back but, in the end, he had to. By the time he got back Patsy was asleep and dawn was just about break. He lay on the bed thinking about Zella. He couldn't seem to rid her from his mind.

When they went down for breakfast the next morning, Patsy looked angrily at him.

"I'm sorry about last night, Patsy."

"I don't understand what's going on."

"You don't need to. Tell you what, how about we go visit the Central Pier today?" desperately trying to change the subject.

"O-K... That could be fun."

"We could go on the beach, then get some lunch?"

After lunch they went to tower ballroom.

Patsy smiled. "OK, you are forgiven."

"Phew..."

He smiled, he had managed to smooth things over for the moment, but he didn't know how he was going to do this long term. He didn't love Patsy and he never would.

Chapter 16

As soon as Zella and Clive arrived home he wanted to her to tell him everything about her and Alden.

"We can discuss this later."

"No… now!"

"But there nothing to tell, really"

"I think there is. I heard him tell you he still loved you and the marriage to your sister is a mistake."

"But …"

"Zella… **NOW!**" His voice became loud and angry.

"OK…"

She sat him down and told him the whole story. He looked at her, puzzled and confused. He needed to know how she felt about Alden now.

"Nothing… I feel nothing."

"Are you lying?"

"No… I love *you*, Clive. Why would I have married you if I still had feelings for Alden?"

"I don't know"

"I love you."

"Prove it."

"Sorry, I don't understand."

"I want us to have a baby. If you really love me, you will have my baby."

"Yes, I want to have children."

"Well then... Now! I don't mean in a few years like we talked about, I mean *now*."

"Alright, we will have a baby."

"No time like the present." Clive smiled a cold, hard smile and grabbed her hand.

She didn't like the way he was behaving and told him to let her go. He demand she go upstairs and when she told him to stop he started pulling her toward the stairs.

"Stop it!" She shouted.

"Zella, I'll get the idea that there *is* something going on with you and Alden if you don't come now."

"I will not be bullied. I *will* have a baby but you will not blackmail me into it, Clive."

Clive crumpled. He sat down putting his head in his hand and told her he was sorry.

"I just got jealous, that's all."

"It's alright."

"I do still want to try for a baby though.

"So do I..."

She moved over to kiss him. He put his arms round her and held her tight. He didn't like the fact that she had loved Alden so much and he felt threatened. He knew Alden wanted Zella back.

Derick also had some smoothing over to do with Bessie. She told him she had overheard his remark and that's why she had been off with him since the wedding. He swore he hadn't meant to upset her.

"Derick, do you want children?"

"Yeah… but definitely not yet."

"That's alright. I understand that."

"Why?"

"Because, Derick… it's always better to get these things up front then everyone knows where they stand."

"Yeah, I couldn't agree more."

He thought, however, that there was more to this conversation than met the eye and decided to buy a ring as he felt she had something to tell him but didn't know how. And he was right. Bessie was, in fact, pregnant and now she knew what Derick's thoughts were, she knew what she had to do.

Her friend Glenda knew someone who could help her but it would cost her money. A few days later, Glenda took Bessie to her 'friend'. As she walked into the front room, he asked for the money upfront and told her to take her panties off and lay on the bed. The bed was covered with a white sheet which was at least clean. He started and she felt a sharp jab. After a while, he told her to go home and warned her to expect some cramps to follow.

On their way home, Bessie started feeling nauseous and experienced increasingly bad pelvic cramps. Glenda got her home and told her to go to bed because what she was feeling was normal, she said that she had been to the same place the month before. Then she left.

As Bessie lies in her bed the cramps became intolerable and she began losing blood. With the room spinning about her,she drifted off and lost consciousness. When her mother went to wake her the next morning she screamed a heart wrenching scream and Bessie's dad rushed in. Their daughter was dead, she'd haemorrhaged in the night. Horrified by the amount of blood on the bed, Bessie's dad ran to the telephone box at the end of the street to call the doctor. When the doctor arrived, he confirmed the worst. Her mother fell to the floor crying uncontrollably while her dad broke down in spite of his efforts to stay strong..

As Derick walked down the street he saw the coroner's van at Bessie's house and sped up as he wondered what had happened. He arrived at the gate just as they were bringing Bessie's body out. He looked wordlessly from Bessie's dad to her mum but they shook their heads. Bessie's dad took Derick inside to tell him Bessie had passed away.

"No... no... I was going to ask her to marry me no... this, no..."

"I'm sorry, Derick."

"What happened?"

"We're not sure yet."

Derick gave him the ring and asked him to put it on her finger. He wanted her to wear his ring always. He walked to the telephone box in a daze. It hadn't registered with him at all what had happened. He called Alden but broke down as he tried to tell him what had happened.

"I need you, Al."

"Where are you?"

"The telephone box on Bessie's street."

"OK I'm on my way."

By the time Alden got there, Derick was sat on a wall, sobbing,

"What on Earth's happened?"

"Bessie's dead."

"*WHAT?*"

"She's dead. I think she aborted our baby and it's all gone horribly wrong."

"Did you tell her to do this, D?"

"No! She hadn't even told me she was pregnant although I kinda guessed. I was going to marry her, you know. Why would she do this?"

"Come on. Let's get you home."

At the funeral Derick was distraught. He blamed himself. He felt he had given her the wrong answers to the question she'd asked him that day. When Bessie's mum asked if he knew what she was going to do he swore he didn't, otherwise he would have talked her out of it.

"Why didn't she tell me?"

"I don't know." Alden said.

"She should have told me."

"Maybe…"

Alden knew Bessie's death was going to weigh heavily on Derick's mind for a long time to come.

Chapter 17

Pasty and Alden had been married a couple of months and there was no denying she was a good wife. She was happy and married to the man she loved. She was telling Mary how happy she was.

"All I have to do now is get pregnant."

"Patsy? There's no baby? But you told Alden…"

"Yeah… yeah… yeah …I know what I told him."

"But…that's so *wrong!*" Mary didn't like the way Patsy had tricked Alden.

"It will happen soon."

"You don't know that, Patsy"

"Yes I do."

Mary was so disappointed in her: how could she do such a wicked thing? She didn't like how selfish and underhand she had become

What they didn't know was that Alden had come home early and he'd overheard what Patsy had said. He suddenly appeared at the kitchen door and glared at then both. Patsy hung her head, knowing he had heard everything.

"Go home, Mary."

Mary looked at Patsy. Patsy nodded and told her to go, she'd be OK.

"So, there's no baby?"

"Alden... I..."

"You lied to me, you tricked me. Have you any idea what it's like being married to someone you don't love?"

"I love you..."

His voice became louder, he was really angry

"I don't love you, I lost the woman I loved because of you."

"Oh, is that right? Well, where the fuck is she then?"

"She's married."

"I knew it! She's a married women, cheating on her husband with you. Are you still sleeping with her?... because that would explain the lack of sex in this house."

"What? NO! What the fuck are you talking about? She wasn't married before... that came after she heard about you and your fucking crush."

"Well, if she loved you she would be with you now,"

"I have had it with you! I'm leaving. You disgust me... there are no words for you!"

"You can't leave me, Alden."

He told her he could and would. She told him if he left her she would tell her mother that she was pregnant and he had made her lose it.

"Go ahead..."

"Zella was right to dislike you."

"What d'ya mean?" He thought of Zella and how she would hate him even more if Patsy told her that. "What the fuck is wrong with you?"

"I love you…"

"I don't love you. Why … why would you love someone who loves someone else?"

He was in a nightmare, his life unravelling before his eyes How the hell did he get here, and how the hell will he get out? It had been the worst day of his life when he met Patsy. He didn't know what to do, he had to think. Patsy, however, already had a backup ready. She spoke to Zella the next day and told her she'd been pregnant but had lost her baby. Zella had to pretend she didn't know about the pregnancy. Patsy was really convincing, crying hysterically down the phone.

"I'm so sorry, Patsy. Does mum know?"

"No. Please don't tell her, it will only upset her."

Patsy convinced Zella to keep quiet. She then informed Alden that she had told Zella about losing the baby

"What baby? There is no fucking baby! Why would you do that?"

Alden didn't wait for an answer. He stormed out of the house and headed straight to Derick's. When he came to the door, Alden told him to get his coat on.

"Al… What's wrong?"

"That fucking woman!"

"Patsy? What has she done?"

"She's not pregnant, never has been…"

"What you mean, 'she's not pregnant'?"

"It was all made up, she made it up to trap me…"

"Fuck me Alden. Are you throwing her out?"

"Ohhhh, I'm sorry bud, you don't need this at the moment, I'll go"

"Al, it's alright."

As they made their way to the pub, Alden explained everything – about the woman he loved and how she had got the wrong impression about him and Patsy. Derick was shocked and told himself he'd had a narrow escape. This could very easily have been him.

Alden got very drunk that night and crashed out on Derick's sofa. He kept mumbling, *'Zella's going to hate me'*. Derick had had a fair few drinks himself and didn't quite understand what Zella had to do with this.

"She'll be sorry she fucked with me"

"Shit… don't tell me if you're going to kill her… I don't want to beeee," he hiccoughed violently in mid-sentence, "an… an… accomplish… *accomplice* even." Then he hiccoughed again and laughed loudly.

"We could kill her together!" Alden spat out, laughing hysterically.

Derick was laughing so much he could barely speak, "Noooooo, Noooooo…" then he passed out on the floor.

"Derickkkkkk… Talk to me, buddy. You're not dead are youuuuuuu?"

Alden leant over and looked down at him. Hearing him snoring, he smiled drunkenly.

"You're *not* dead, you drunken bastard. You're just a pissssss head who can't hold his liquor."

And with that he passed out as well.

❧ ❧

Meanwhile, in London, Clive was getting increasingly frustrated they had not got pregnant yet. In his disappointment, he made a comment that offended Zella. He implied that she had a problem with getting pregnant.

"It could be *you* Clive, have you thought of that?"

"It's not me!"

"Well, it could be that we are trying too hard."

"You just want a career."

"I never said that."

"Or… maybe I'm the wrong man." He spewed out sarcastically.

"Don't start that again."

He was jealous of her career or anyone who took any interest in her, especially Alden, that name just brought out the bile in him. He still couldn't get over what he'd heard that night, he had it in his head that there was still something between Zella and Alden. His response was to become very controlling, wanting to know her every movement. It was damaging the way she felt about him and she wasn't prepared to risk destroying her career either. They were drifting apart fast. It didn't help when he had a night out with his friends and came home rolling drunk. His drinking was getting worse and she didn't know how to cope with him. He was aggressive and rough when he had a drink. She had become unhappy with her marriage but wasn't sure how to change it. She suspected he was sleeping other women, she often smelt them on his clothes, their perfume lingering on him. She felt utterly betrayed.

Zella was getting sick of him behaving so childishly and foolishly she told him so. He didn't like it and in his drunken state he lashed out at her, cutting her lip. She was shocked he had hit her. She couldn't bear to look at him the next morning, he had disappointed her so much. He woke late the next morning to find she'd already left for work. He didn't know what to do, he felt so bad. He'd never raised his hand to any woman before, and it was Zella, Zella he'd hurt, he hated himself. As soon as he sobered up he went out to buy flowers and chocolates for when she got home.

"Zella, I'm so sorry. Please forgive me."

"Just leave me alone."

Not long after that, Clive disappeared for a day. It turned out that he had gone to Chesterfield to see Alden. He struggled to track him down and was on the point of leaving when he spotted him. He was stood with a woman, she seemed to be running her fingers through his hair... and it wasn't Patsy that was for sure. Clive waited and watched as the woman kissed him seductively while Alden seemed to respond as eagerly. Finally she walked away as Alden watched. Preoccupied with this very elegant lady he didn't see Clive approach him before tapping him on the shoulder.

"Have you no shame?" Clive said, getting on his moral high horse.

"Clive...what are you doing here?"

"Who was she?"

"That's none of your business."

"I don't give a shit really."

"What are you doing here then?

133

"Stay away from Zella"

He was being quite threatening, pushing his finger hard into Alden's chest.

"You told her you loved her!" He screeched as he prodded him.

Alden grabbed his finger and bent it back.

"Get out of my face, Clive! You have no idea what that was or why I said it!"

"Oh… I fucking *do!*"

Alden moved forward, pushing his face into Clive's,
"No… you …fucking… *DON'T"*

"You get out of my fucking face."

"Or… what?"

"Just stay away from Zella, otherwise Patsy finds out about you and her"

Clive congratulated himself that Alden wouldn't want that – he wouldn't want to hurt Zella in any way.

"You have no idea what Zella means to me. She was my girl first and you know what they say about first loves, they never really go away."

Clive was seething with unease. His nostrils began to flare, his eyes narrowed and his patience was running thin.

"Just… just stay the fuck away from her!" He blustered.

Alden smiled and knew he had got under his skin.

He didn't care about Clive but he did care about Zella and he wasn't going to do anything to hurt her. He would take his time and work out how to win her back. He was going to sort this mess out and be with the woman he loved so much. He didn't know how… but he would do it *somehow*.

Chapter 18

1959

The final straw came when Zella and Clive attended a charity fashion show with Carlos and Miriam. Zella was having a great time discussing work with other designers. Dorian Fabron wanted to work with Zella and asked her if she would consider working alongside him. She jumped at the chance. It would be another a big opportunity for her. Clive, however, was getting bored and irritated. Carlos made it worse unknowingly when he happened to mention Alden. Carlos was taking professionally but Clive didn't see it that way and jumped to conclusions.

"What?"

"I just said they'd make a good team…"

Clive exploded and stormed over to Zella, grabbing her arm forcefully. He yanked her away from her conversation with Dorian.

"What the hell are you doing?"

"We're going home."

"No…"

"Yes, Zella, we are!"

He made an awful scene, shouting at her in front of all those people, not to mention her boss. She was so embarrassed and apologised to Dorian and Carlos. They told her it was OK but it wasn't for her, it was unforgivable. She thought Clive's outburst had cost her chance to work with Dorian Fabron.

When they arrived home she went straight up stairs and started to pack. She'd had enough of his womanising, his suspicious outbursts and accusations.

"What are you doing?"

"I'm leaving."

"No… No, Zella," He went from being sorry to angry again, shouting "You want to be with *him*, don't you?"

"I can't do this anymore; I don't *want* to do this anymore."

"Please, Zella."

"You may have just lost me a wonderful opportunity"

"Zella, wait I have something for you. I was saving it, but you can have it now."

"I don't want anything from you." She shouted as he ran from the room.

She had called a taxi while he was away. When he came back he handed her a small box.

"Clive…" She pushed the box back towards him.

"Zella, take the fucking box."

"I don't want it… my taxi will be here in a moment."

In his rage he grabbed the phone and ripped it right out of the wall.

"NO!" He shouted

It took her all her effort to make her way to the door.

He grabbed her arm. "You'll get *nothing*."

"I don't want anything."

"I can have my pick of women. In fact, I've had other women… You're just useless, you can't even give me a baby. You're frigid, there no fun in fucking you, *I don't need you!*"

Zella closed her eyes and sighed. She just wanted to get out of there, he was getting more and more aggressive. She told him she would have the rest of her stuff picked up.

Clive was so angry he ran upstairs, scooped up the rest of her stuff and threw it out of the window. Pulling out his lighter, he ran outside and set it all on fire.

"It's all on fucking fire… no need to come back for anything"

Zella quickly grabbed the bags she had packed and ran outside. Luckily the taxi had just pulled up and she gave the driver Carlos's address. She couldn't believe Clive had done that, it really was the final straw.

Carlos and Miriam hadn't got back when she arrived there so she sat on the step waiting for them. When they pulled up they saw her sat there sobbing, mascara running down her cheeks. Her lips quivered as she told them what had happened. They took her inside and Miriam made some tea.

"Drink that, sweetheart." She said, handing her a cup.

"Thank you, Miriam."

"You're welcome."

"If I could just stay here tonight then tomorrow I can find somewhere to go."

She was feeling as if her world had come crashing down on top of her. Miriam told her she could stay as long as she need to.

ॐ ॐ

Over the coming weeks she found a small flat, nothing special. Carlos helped with that and in put her in touch with a fantastic solicitor who had represented him in his own divorce four years ago. Carlos made the introductions for her and the wheels were put in motion. She also wrote to her mum to let her know what had happened. Florence immediately wanted to be there for her, she caught the next train to London.

"What happened, darling?"

"He was jealous."

"About… what…?"

"Everything, I think."

"Alden?"

"Alden… Why Alden?"

"Zella, I know how Alden feels about you. I've known for a while… I see the way he looks at you."

"No… Mum, you've got that all wrong."

Florence shook her head. She knew the feeling was mutual, she could see it in her daughter's eyes.

"Why don't you come home, Zella?"

"My job is here, Mum."

"I worry about you…"

"I'm fine, really."

Florence stayed in London with her daughter for a few days to make she was alright and looking after herself. Zella told her she shouldn't be worrying about either of them anymore, she should be enjoying her life. She had been a wonderful mother and now it was time for her to live her life. Florence snorted and told her that she would always worry about her girls.

In the meantime, Dorian had been in touch with Carlos about teaming up with Zella and arranged a meeting. He took her out for lunch and showed her some of his designs. She was like a kid in a sweet shop, bewildered by the colours and styles. She sat motionless and wide-eyed, she could scarcely believe what she was seeing.

"These are *amazing!*

Dorian smiled. "You like?" He said in his beautiful French accent.

"Oh yes... I like very much."

"Excellent... I would like you to come to Paris...Yes?"

"I'd love to."

"I can show you more when you come over."

"I can't wait"

"I will, hmmm... *arrange* it."

"OHHHH, Yes please."

She set about organising her passport and worked hard on some ideas and came up with some new designs along the same lines as Dorian's to show him when she went to Paris. Carlos was delighted for her and told her she had been born for this. She smiled and told him that if it hadn't been for him, none of this would be happening for her.

"You deserve it, you work hard."

A few weeks later Dorian called Zella with all the arrangements for her visit. She was so excited it hadn't crossed her mind she would be alone. She wasn't the type to let that stand in her way, though. She knew what she wanted and was confident being on her own, although she was sure that Dorian would be there to show her around.

Paris

She arrived at the airport not sure exactly what she was supposed to do next. A kindly lady pointed out where she was supposed to go to check in. She checked in successfully and headed to the departure lounge where she bought herself a cup of tea and waited for her flight to be called.

As she boarded the aircraft she smiled quietly to herself. She couldn't believe she was actually doing this, it had only ever been a dream but here she was, on her way to Paris. She was excited and nervous all at the same time. As they took off, she felt like an eagle soaring though the sky. She settled back in her seat and watched the clouds drift by. How tiny everything looked from up here, she thought it was *amazing.*

The plane started its descent and there was the excitement and nerves again, her heart fluttering as the wheels touched the tarmac. She made her way to passport control and grabbed her case to go through Customs. Outside, she flagged a taxi and made her way to her hotel. Checking in was a little difficult as she didn't speak any French. First things first, she settled into her room then waited for Dorian to call, to arrange to come and get her. He told her to wait in the foyer and he would meet her there.

"Mademoiselle Zella"

"Dorian, how lovely to see you."

"*Merci*"

"I need to learn some French I think.

Dorian laughed. "Shall we?"

He escorted her to his car and drove to his office first, to show her some of his designs. Everything he showed her was so chic, barrelled and fitted, but when she saw the dresses that draped, she sat there with her mouth open.

"Well, *Cherie*,What do you think?"

"I love them, I love them all."

Dorian smiled proudly. "Let me see your designs now Zella?"

She handed them over and waited with baited breath. He, on the other hand, was taking his time looking at each design. She was on the edge of her seat waiting to hear what he thought,

"Hmmm..." He muttered.

'He doesn't like them,' she thought to herself

"I can do some more if these are not good enough..."

"I like them, *Cherie*."

"Phew..." She sighed heavily.

"Yes... I like them."

"You do?"

He nodded, looking up at her, "Yes, I do."

She was so relieved. She had worried that Clive had ruined this for her and she had been so looking forward to working with Dorian.

That evening, Dorian took her to the *Moulin Rouge*. She had never seen anything like it in her life, it was simply amazing. She settled back in her seat and soaked up the atmosphere.

"I must take you to Notre Dame."

"Wonderful! Can I see the Eiffel Tower too, before I go home?"

"But of course…"

The next day they went to Notre Dame and climbed the bell tower. She soaked up all its history, it was quite simply a masterpiece. Later, Dorian took her to the Eiffel Tower. He proudly gave her its history, how it had been built for the great Paris Exhibition.

"Oh My, 1889? The view must be *spectacular*."

"Would you like to go up?"

"Oh yes…"

The view was amazing, out of this world. She took what seemed like hundreds of pictures of all that she saw. She'd had the best day and was sorry she didn't have time to see more. She had an early flight the following day so she needed to sleep. Next morning, Dorian insisted on driving her to the airport. He told her that next time he would take her to some more special places. She told him how much she looked forward to it.

When she arrived back in London, a letter from her solicitor informed her that Clive had rushed his side of the divorce through and there were just some formalities to go through. She was virtually a single woman again. Divorce was not a common thing and she couldn't help but feel a little sad that her marriage had ended, just like that.

Chapter 19

1960

Alden was at his desk going through some paperwork when his phone rang.

"Am I talking to Alden Pearce?"

"Yes… Who…"

"Hello, I'm Kenneth Carter from *Weekly Whisper*."

"Oh, Hi…"

"Alden, I have been looking at some of your work and I'm very impressed."

"Thank you."

"I would like to meet with you to discuss your future."

"Wow! Yes, I would like that"

"Shall we say 1:30pm tomorrow at?"

"Yes… Thank you Mr Carter"

Alden was feeling rather proud of himself, the one and only Mr Carter wanted to meet him. The *Weekly Whisper* went worldwide – if he could get on Carter's team he would get to travel the world and meet the rich and famous.

At Lunch

After some smalltalk, Carter told Alden he wanted him on his team, then he went on to tell him about Dorian Fabron's new collection.

"My information is that he's teamed up with an unknown designer."

"Oh right... Who?"

"A... Zella Russell."

"Zella Russell...Really?"

"Do you know her?"

"Yes, she's my..." He paused a moment," ...Yeah, I know her."

"This is good, Alden."

"It is?"

"I would like to offer you a job at *Weekly Whisper*."

"That's fantastic... thank you Mr Carter"

Stan was sorry to lose Alden but he knew one day he would have to let him go. Alden was a great reporter, he always got his story and Stan knew he was destined for bigger things. Derick was sad to see his buddy go but he too was happy for him.

"Give me some time D and I'll get you in as my camera man."

"Al, that would be great."

❧ ❧

144

The following week, Alden was given his first assignment. He was in London, to interview Michael Charles while he was covering his photo shoot. Michael Charles was the photographer who discovered Marlene May and made her in to a worldwide model. Alden was having the time of his life. He was away from Patsy for months at a time, he was covering all the latest fashions and he got to hang out with the models. He even managed a bit of a fling with one of them and he made no secret of it either.

Alden admired Michael's technique. He had a natural way of bringing the best out in all his models , getting them in to the pose that was best for them and away his camera went, the lens juddered, flash... flash... flash, click...click... click a whirring noise. Models loved posing for Michael.

Soon, Alden got to hang out with Michael and they would go out in the evenings with the models.

Michael attracted all the models with his unlined baby face, high cheek bones natural blonde hair and emerald green eyes, Alden did notice that Michael never stayed with one model for more than one night. There were rumours about him and Marlene May, that they had once been married. Alden had yet to hear the full story but what a scoop it would be if he could.

Times were changing. Alden was covering womenswear, menswear, autumn and springwear. Model appeared in ruffles, fun prints, very flamboyant looks, bright and bold colours. The media had new technology, Television now provided a role for the models and designers. Teenagers were becoming more interested in clothes, many celebrities started wearing designer clothes. It created more opportunities for fashion than ever before. The 60s would be a life changing decade. Beehives gave way to shorter styles, even mens hair styles changed with 'mop top' styles after their favourite bands. Oh yes times were changing, both Zella and Alden were excited about their futures.

❧ ❧

When Alden arrived back home, Patsy was in a foul mood. She had convinced herself that Alden had been with his mystery woman and, more to the point, she was convinced she was one of the models.

"You've been with her, haven't you?"

"Patsy, I'm not having this conversation again."

She slapped him hard across the face leaving a big red hand print on his cheek.

"I don't want you with her."

"You've got want you wanted… we are married, let's leave it at that."

"I want you to want *me*"

"I don't," he snarled callously, "I don't want you in any way at all!"

"I love you Alden, please love me back." She said, trying to pull him close.

"Do you know how pathetic you sound?"

Alden walked away from her to get changed. He was attending a dinner meeting with Kenneth and the rest of the team.

"Don't walk away from me!"

"Patsy… give it up."

Patsy hurled the nearest thing she could find at him, missing him by inches. He turned back and grabbed her by the shoulders.

"You are nothing to me, *nothing*... do you understand?"

He got changed and headed out of the door without a backward glance or a word said.

Dinner party at the *Tower Bass* restaurant

Alden was having a grand old time circulating the room, chitchatting with everyone and gathering snatches of all the conversations going on.

"I hear that Dorian Fabron is having his collection shown in Paris, Milan and London this year"

"Really?"

"Yes, I believe that Zella Russell is going to Paris to join him."

Alden's ears pricked up at that. It was the second time he'd heard Zella's name in connection with the show and determined to asks if he could cover the Paris event, Kenneth had already decided he was the right man to send but was curious why he was so eager to go.

"I think it's a great opportunity."

"What about Milan and London, do you want to cover those too?"

"Yes, of course"

Kenneth liked Alden. He was eager and hungry to cover all the new stories and he saw a bright future for him. When Alden finally got home that night he'd had a lot to drink and was a little worse for wear. Patsy was lying in wait for him.

"Where have you been till this hour?"

"You *know* where I have been."

"Why are you so late?"

"Fuck off, Patsy!"

"Don't swear at me, it's not what husbands do, they don't use language like that to their wife"

"*What?* A wife doesn't trick her husband into being with her by pretending to be pregnant. I don't give a shit what you like or dislike, Patsy."

He told her he was going to Paris, possibly Milan and London, so she could do whatever she wanted, he simply didn't care.

Patsy knew Zella was going to Paris. Didn't that mean he couldn't be with that woman? How could he when Zella would be there, keeping her eye on him? When she pointed this out to him, he just laughed knowingly.

"Why are you laughing?

He continued to laugh, making her angrier and angrier because he wouldn't tell her why he found that so funny.

"Go to bed, Patsy."

Patsy stormed off, slamming the bedroom door to. She knew he wasn't going to follow, he would sleep on the couch as he had so many times since they had been married. He refused to be in the same bed as her, but even so she still felt that she could make him fall in love with her. She just wanted to show him what a loving wife she could be.

Chapter 20

Paris Fashion, 1961

Zella received her ticket to go to Paris to show her collection with Dorian, little knowing that Alden would be there covering it. Alden himself was excited, looking forward to the trip. He couldn't wait to see Zella now that Clive was out of the picture and he was also looking forward to seeing her collection.

The following morning, Alden brought his case down and headed out of the door without even saying goodbye to Patsy. He was hoping he would be on the same flight as Zella and wanted to get to the airport early but she must have been on the flight before as he did not see her at all. Patsy was still confident that Alden would have to be on his best behaviour,

In Paris, Zella had arrived at the hotel, unpacked and walked round the shops. She took in all the sights around her, wandering in and out of clothes shops taking note of all the designs she saw. She stopped at a little café and

ordered a croissant and a coffee and sat admiring the view
around her then made her way back to the hotel. She
stopped at reception to book a table for dinner

"A table for one, *S'il vous plaît*."

"Of course, *mademoiselle*."

"*Une table pour deux, s'il vous plaît*." echoed a voice from
 behind her.

"*Bien sûr, monsieur*."

"*Merci beaucoup*."

Zella turned, only to come face to face with Alden

"Alden… what are you doing here?"

"I'm covering the fashion show."

"Is Patsy with you?"

"No…"

"Oh…." Her mind went into overdrive.

The waiter interrupted her train of thought, "*Votre table est
prête, monsieur*."

"*Merci beaucoup*… our table will is booked for 7:30pm."

"*Our* table…?"

"Yes…"

At 7:30pm Alden waited for Zella to come down and the
waiter led them to their table. He asked if they would like a
drink to start with and Alden ordered a bottle of
Chardonnay, Zella felt very guilty, as if she was doing
something wrong sitting there with her sister's husband,
her ex-lover. Alden assured her that there was nothing
wrong with the two of them having dinner together.

"You look very beautiful tonight."

"Thank you, but please don't do that."

"Why?"

"Just don't, Alden."

"What would you like to talk about then?"

"Anything but what happened with us…. Patsy, talk about Patsy."

"I don't want to talk about your sister."

"Talk about the fashion show, then…" she said abruptly, feeling flustered.

They made small talk. Zella talked about her designs and told him she was really looking forward to the week ahead. Alden just sat and listened to her, looking deep into her eyes, watching her lips as she spoke, hanging on every word she said. Oh how he loved this woman, he needed her back in his life.

He lay in his bed that night thinking about her, imagining holding her, touching her, the feel of her skin, kissing her lips. He just wanted to go to her and make love to her, she was his forbidden love.

He was not the only one thinking about how thing used to be. Zella found herself imagining him making love to her like he had all that time ago, the way he caressed her body, the way he made her feel, all those memories flooding back. She had to stop this, she was scared she would let her feelings show. She *couldn't*, she *shouldn't* feel like this. She tossed and turned but she couldn't get him out of her head. She finally fell asleep but only to dream of Alden.

The next morning she tried to avoid him and thought she was doing quite well until Dorian walked in with Alden in tow. She turned aside to avoid eye contact with him but it was too late and he was making his way over.

"Zella… good morning."

"Good morning."

"I was thinking perhaps we could have dinner again tonight."

"We did that last night, Alden."

"And we could do it again tonight."

"I don't know."

"Why…? What are you scared of?"

She took a deep breath. "Nothing… nothing at all."

"Shall we say eight, then?"

"Yes, fine."

Alden knew he was getting to her from her reluctance to be alone with him. She was frightened she might not be able to hold back. The way she looked at him he knew she still loved him.

That evening Zella made her way down to the lobby where Alden was waiting for her. He looked so handsome in a black shirt and trousers with a black jacket, his hair slicked back just like Alvin Preston. Zella stopped in her tracks. *'I can't do this,'* she thought. She was about to turn back to her room when he spotted her and called her name. She had to go over, walking slowly toward him. He smiled. *'Oh no, that smile,'* she mumbled to herself.

"Would you like a drink?" He asked.

"Yes, please."

He ordered her a glass of wine which downed in one, she was nervous.

"My…. Were you thirsty?"

"Yes… I think we should go and eat, don't you?"

"What's your rush?"

"I'm hungry…"

"Anyone would think you want to get dinner over with."

"No… just hungry."

As they waited for their meal, he began to stare at her, making her even more nervous. After dinner he suggested they take a stroll.

"Yes… why not, I'll go get my coat" she thought this would be better than sitting there starring at each other

He smiles holding his hand out

"What are you doing?"

"Helping you from your chair.

"It's alright, you don't have to."

"I want to."

He took her hand then pulled her toward him. "I…love …I mean you look beautiful tonight."

Zella swallowed hard. "I'll get my coat" She said nervously.

When she came back, Alden helped her with her coat then they went for a stroll along the Invalides Bridge. She remembered how exciting and fun he was and just how charming he was, he could charm the birds right out of the trees. As they strolled there was a street violinist playing. As they approached the centre of the bridge, Alden took hold of her and waltzed her round. He sang to her, making his own word up as he went along and she laughed as he spun her round. An elderly couple remarked on how much in love they looked. "Yes, Yes… I'm very much in love," Alden shouted. The lady took hold of Zella's hand, "You have the look of love in your eyes, my dear," she whispered to her in a beautiful French accent. Zella just smiled then moved away from Alden, suddenly going very quiet

"What's wrong?"

"We need to head back to the hotel. It's an early start tomorrow."

She started walking towards the hotel but Alden grabbed her arm and pulled her back.

"What's wrong?"

"Nothing."

"Yes there is… What did that lady say to you?"

"Nothing…"

He pulled her to him. Looking into her eyes he told her he loved her. She put her head down shaking it and told him this was wrong. He lifted her head with his finger under her chin.

"Zella, I love you."

She stared at him intently for a moment. Gently, his head moved towards her. He was about to kiss her, their lips inches away from each other before she pulled away.

"No, Alden. This is so wrong."

Zella hardly said a word as they headed back to the hotel.

"Would you like a nightcap?" Alden asked.

"No thank you."

"I'll see you to you room."

"You don't have to do that."

"Please Zella… I want to."

She really didn't want him to but he insisted and they made their way to the lift. He pressed the lift button then stood silently staring at her. When the lift reached Zella's floor she stepped out to find that Alden was right behind her to escort her to her room.

"Goodnight, Alden."

"Good night, Zella."

Zella backed in to her room, looking intently at him as she shut the door. She pressed her head against it, little knowing he was still there on the other side, his head pressed against the other side of the door. Finally, he stepped back and walked to the lift. As the doors opened he looked down the corridor then stepped in. The doors were about to close when he got out, paced the corridor for a few minutes, then made his way back to Zella's room. He stood outside the door, he couldn't just walk away he wanted her so much. What he didn't know was that Zella was pacing the floor inside, contemplating opening her door and chasing after him then deciding against it at the last minute. She knew that if she had the inevitable would have happened, their feelings were running so high.

Bright and early the next morning Alden knocked on Zella's door but there was no answer. Zella had got up at the crack of dawn and was already in the dining room having breakfast when Alden got there.

"Morning…"

"Morning, Alden."

"May I join you?"

"Yes, of course."

"Zella… have I upset you?"

"No… Why would you think that?"

He mentioned the previous night. She told him she had just been tired, she had just needed a good night's sleep. He knew it wasn't that, it had something to do with what the elderly lady had whispered in her ear.

"As long as that's all it was."

"I'm fine. I have to leave now, Alden. I need to see Dorian."

"Oh Right… see you later then?"

"Perhaps… I'm rather busy today."

"Yeah… me too."

It was the last day of the fashion show and, for the most part, Zella had managed to stay out of Alden's way. They would be making their way home tomorrow. It had been a wonderful experience but manic, the fashion collection got a good response from the audience and with Alden covering it would have a fantastic write up. Zella had been on the go since she arrived and, of course, there was the emotional upset, she could have done without that. She thought she would have to get used to seeing Alden at these events, he was a reporter after all.

Alden asked Zella to spend their last day together. She wasn't sure it was really the best idea but she agreed, somehow she couldn't help herself. They went to lunch at a little bistro he'd found, then went for a walk along the river Seine. Alden didn't want to go home, he wished he could just stay in Paris with Zella. He was desperate to explain what had happened with Patsy. He had tried so many times.

"Why won't you let me tell you what happened?"

"What does it matter now, you are married to my sister."

"It matters a great deal, Zella."

"Please don't, Alden."

He could see how much he was upsetting her. That wasn't his intention, so he simply told her he'd leave it for the present.

"No... *forever*, Alden. I don't want to know!"

Alden didn't understand. Did it make it easier for her, could it change things, or maybe it would make things worse? He had only just got her to speak to him again, he thought that would just have to do for now.

Chapter 21

The trip to the Paris with Dorian had drawn the attention of Ingrid Halvorson and she was very interested in meeting Zella. She liked what she had done with Dorian and wanted to know if she fancied teaming up with her for her next collection in Milan, if she was free. A fresh pair of eyes, fresh ideas were always good. She was intrigued to know what Zella would come up with.

"I would love to."

"Well, I wasn't sure if you would be in Milan with Dorian."

"Dorian already had his collection for Milan. He did ask me to go to London, though."

"That's fabulous, I get you for Milan then."

Zella smiled, she was so excited about all the offers she was getting. She got to develop some ideas she had and it was very good for Carlos as well as he got to make all Zella's creations.

Ingrid asked her to call in at her office and told her if she had any current designs to bring them with her. The following week she made her way to Ingrid's office. She was stepping into the lift when a shout stopped her.

"Hold on, let me in."

Zella held the door and a young man piled in. He was loaded up with photographic equipment, cameras, stands and bags of film draped over his shoulders. He didn't speak, no thank you for holding the door or anything, which Zella thought was quite rude. He looked her up and down and when the lift doors opened he turned and said, *"After you."*

Zella made a point of saying thank you and he went one way while she went the other. She shrugged her shoulders. "Ah well," she muttered to herself.

She headed to the reception deck and asked for Ingrid. A few moments later she came out of her office.

"Zella, how nice to see you. Please tell me you have brought some designs with you."

"Yes…"

"Magnificent"

Ingrid looked at Zella's designs and, after what could only have been a few minutes but seemed like hours, she looked up and smiled.

"These are wonderful. Carlos has told me all about you."

A wide grin swept across Zella's face.

"Thank you."

"I want these designs for the collection in Milan. What do you think?"

"Yes, that's brilliant"

"That's a deal then… we team up!"

"It certainly is. Thank you so much."

159

"Dorian loved you. He told me he can't wait to see what you come up with for London but he can't have you this time – I've snapped you up."

Zella smiled, she felt so good and so proud of herself. They shook hands and Ingrid gave her a peck on the cheek and told her she would see her soon. Zella headed back to the lift and bumped into the young man who had been so rude in the lift earlier. As the doors opened they both stepped in. Michael, the young man, looked at her and said, "Would you like to go for a drink?" 'Cheeky,' she thought, he couldn't say thank you but he had the nerve to ask her out for a drink. She was taken back for a moment then said 'Yes'. She could hardly say 'No' as she couldn't resist his big emerald eyes and that baby face.

They headed to a bar not far from the river Thames and Michael ordered a bottle of red wine.

"Now… my name is Michael, Michael Charles. What's yours?"

"Zella… Russell"

"Zella…Zella… Zella. I love that name."

"Thank you."

He asked what she was doing at Ingrid's office, was she going to be a new model?

"No…" She smiled. "I'm going to be working with Ingrid on her new collection."

"Oh… you're a designer?"

"Yes… What do you do?"

"I'm Ingrid's photographer, I get to take photographs of beautiful women. I've never heard of you… Sorry."

"Don't be… I'm not a *famous* designer"

"You could be a model"

"Oh… you are very good." She laughed.

He smiled. He couldn't stop staring at her, she had totally captivated him. He asked her if she would like to go back to his place for a nightcap.

"Why not…."

'How daring am I?' She thought, wondering whether she had done the right thing. She didn't know this man, whatever was she doing?

They flagged a taxi down then headed back to his apartment where he poured them both a brandy. Zella took her jacket off and Michael suddenly reached over, pulling her closer to kiss her. She kissed him back and things started to heat up. The next thing they knew they were pulling at each others' clothes, undressing each other in a fever. Moving his hands over her stomach, up between her breasts, he kissed her harder, deeper, his body pushing against hers. She could feel his throbbing bulge against her thigh. He looked her in the eyes, traced his fingers down her throat and then pushed himself into her. She let out a groan.

"Oh! Yes… Yes…!" He moaned.

"Uh-uh-uh…"

She couldn't catch her breath, it was so hard to breath when he touched her, he excited her so much. As they moved in rhythm he suddenly flipped her over, his fingertips running up her back.

Her heart was pounding, she thought it just might jump out of her chest. As they climaxed Michael's head jerked back, she felt him stiffen up then just flop onto the bed next to her, their hot naked bodies entwined together as they drifted off to sleep.

When she woke the next morning she found Michael staring at her, running his finger over her skin.

"Good morning."

"What time is it?"

"Breakfast time." He kissed her shoulder softly, "It's nine o'clock. Why?"

She jumped up. "Oh no… I've to go. I've a meeting with Carlos at nine thirty."

She got dressed quickly. As she was rushing out, Michael took her hand and asked if he could see her later.

"Yes… I'll call you later." kissing him before she left.

"Zella… you haven't got my number." He shouted.

He quickly scribbled it down, pushing it in her hand. She ran out in a rush she shoved in to her bag. She managed to flag down a taxi and went straight home to get a wash and change her clothes. She arrived twenty minutes late for her meeting.

"Sorry, Carlos."

"Late night, early morning or should I not even ask?"

She rolled her eyes. "Don't ask."

"Fair enough."

Later that day, sat at her desk, she looked for the number Michael had given her but she couldn't find it. 'Oh no,' she thought, 'I've lost it.' She emptied her bag out onto the floor. While she found everything she didn't want, the scrap of paper with his number just wouldn't be found. She was getting more and more upset when Carlos walked and discovered her on her knees panicking.

"What are you doing, Zella?"

"I've lost a number I need. I was in such a rush this morning I pushed it in to my bag, now I've lost it."

"Who was the number for?"

"Michael Charles."

"Fear not, my sweet. I have the number for his secretary."

"Oh Carlos what would I do without you?" She took hold of his face and planted a kiss on his cheek .

"You would be losing important numbers …" He laughed, "Michael Charles hey? Hmmm…"

She looks at him asking what he meant by hmmm! He told her that Michael was a very attractive man and lots of women would chase after him, vying for his attention. He had been married once to a model who was only interested in getting to the top, she broke his heart by leaving when she made it.

"Oh My… who was the model?"

"Marlene May."

"Oh My God, I met her in Paris, she is *so* beautiful."

"Yes… Apparently, he said he would never get married again."

"He is *so* good looking."

"Are you seeing him?"

"We went for a drink last night."

Carlos smiled, "That explains why you were late this morning."

Carlos left her to make her phone call. RING, RING, it seemed ages before his secretary answered.

"Good morning, Michael Charles' office."

"Good morning. Could I speak to Michael, please?"

"Who's calling?"

"Zella Russell."

"Hold the line."

"Zella…"

"Good morning, Michael."

"Good morning and a beautiful one, too."

Straight away, he told her he'd pick her up at the office, not even giving her the chance to go home and change, he would be there at six. His secretary smirked knowingly, she knew him only too well.

At six, Michael picked her up and they went for something to eat before going back to his apartment. Again, their passion for each other was intense. Their kisses were deep and passionate, their hands all over each other, taking each others' clothes off and dropping them as they stumbled to the bed.

It was hot and they were sweating and panting like wild animals as he thrust back and forth, making her groan with pleasure. She felt that glorious feeling of satisfaction when she orgasmed for the second time. She rolled on top of him and moved to the rhythm of his body. Their skin was sticky with sweat. They made love, longer this time, before climaxing again. She lay motionless on top of him as they laboured to catch their breath, finally falling asleep in each others' arms.

The sun began to rise and Zella woke up as it was peeping through the curtains. She quietly got dressed and whispered to her lover on the bed, "I've got to go."

Sleepily, he takes her hand, "Can I see you tonight?"

"I can't, I have a plane to catch."

"When will I see you, I'm away on a location for three days."

"I'll be back in three days." She smiled softly.

"OK… I'll see you when you get back."

"I'll call you"

Michael reached up and pulled her to him to kiss her. Gently and tenderly she kissed him back then reluctantly left.

Chapter 22

Milan

Over in Chesterfield, Alden was packing ready for Derick to pick him up. Derick had joined the team at *Weekly Whisper* by this time and was going to Milan as Alden's camera man, the team was back together.

Patsy hadn't told Alden that Zella would be in Milan, she thought she was going to catch him out. Zella arrived in Milan and went to a little café for something to eat. She made sure she had an early night as she had a lot to do the next day, she was meeting Ingrid to go over the designs.

Early next morning, Zella and Ingrid had breakfast together. They spoke about the show and what was happening. At the same time, the models were all gathering in the lobby so Ingrid and Zella went to meet them all. There, flashing his camera, was Michael. Zella smiled, she was really pleased to see him.

"Hello, I should have known."

"Well, well, well...l if it isn't Miss Russell herself."

"This is your 'location'?"

"Yes… I knew you were here and I wanted to surprise you".

"And you *have*."

"I think we have some unfinished passion to get back to," he whispered in her ear.

She laughed out loud and the models turned and smiled. They knew something was going on with Zella and Michael as he hadn't flirted once with any of them He told Zella he was nearly finished and suggested they spend the rest of the day in bed. This time she giggled. He made her feel giddy and she hadn't felt like that in a long time.

Michael wrapped the shoot up and took Zella's hand leading her towards the lift. As they got in, he pulled her to him, kissing her. Just at that moment, before the doors closed, Alden and Derick arrived. Alden looked round to see Zella with Michael. He saw the passion in that kiss and dropped his case in despair, he couldn't believe what he had just see. He stood with his mouth open looking devastated.

"What wrong with you?"

"No, no, Fuck no… she's with …"

Derick interrupted, "Who …?"

He looked at Alden's stricken face and knew he meant his 'mystery woman' was here.

"No, No, No"

"Alden… get a grip, you are married. You're so lucky to have a wife like Patsy. I'd be so happy if it was me."

"Have you forgotten what she did?"

"Al…"

"She's ruined my fucking life."

"Who is this woman?"

"I can't tell you that."

"Yeah you can. I'm not going to tell Patsy, or anyone else for that matter."

Alden sighed heavily and reluctantly said, " Zella."

"*Zella?*... as in Patsy's sister, Zella...?"

"Yeah..."

"Holly shit... you know how to complicate things, this is not good Alden."

"I was with her when I met Patsy, remember?"

"Yeah... why did you never tell me who she was?"

"I was about to ask Zella to marry me when everything went wrong."

"I still don't understand why you didn't tell me."

"It's long story."

Alden was so upset he avoided Zella as much as he could over the three days. He didn't want anything to do with Michael either.

The fashion show was a great success. People loved Zella's designs so Ingrid was over the moon. She told Zella that they would surely be working together again and, as for Zella, she'd had a fantastic three days being introduced to the fashion world and, of course, having a new lover.

When the show was over, Zella spotted Alden in the hotel restaurant and wondered why she hadn't seen him before. She was relieved in one way but still wondered why.

"Hello, Alden."

"Zella."

"Are you alright?"

"Why, are you bothered?"

"Of course"

He stood up gripped her hand and looked her straight in the eye.

"Are you sleeping with Michael?"

"*What…?* That's none of your business."

"Well, you just answered my question."

He walks past her, bumping into Michael and knocking him flying.

"Morning, Alden."

Alden just walked past him without saying a word.

"What's wrong with him? I didn't know you knew Alden."

"He's my brother in law."

She knew Alden was angry and she felt dreadful Michael asked if she was alright as her face told him she wasn't. She told him she was fine. He suggested they went out for the day seeing as the fashion show had finished and they would be returning tomorrow.

"Yes, let's go out for the day."

Michael took her to the majestic Cathedral. It was an elegant and beautiful building so picturesque, its Gothic architecture shouting out love. They walked to the glamorous *Galleria Vittorio Emanuele II* shopping complex then went to the canal, to a little restaurant on the water's edge. They wandered through the market place there, looking at knick-knacks. She was having a wonderful day.

Michael watched her as she got excited about everything she saw. He had taken his camera with him and took photos of her as she walked.

"Zella…" As she turned, he snapped another picture of her.

"What are you doing?"

"Taking pictures of you."

"Why…?"

"They'll look good in my portfolio."

"Oh I see…"

"Do you know how beautiful you are?"

She blushed as he pulled her gently to him, kissing her tenderly. Taking her hand, they went back to the hotel and it was she who suggested that they go back to his room. Once there, they couldn't leave each other alone and filled the night with passion.

Next day they flew home, there was just the London show to do the following week then Zella would be back to trying to create a new look. She had seen two different designs and wonder if she could come up with something new, combining them both making it her own creation.

Marlene May would be at the London show, she had to look spectacular in one of Zella Russell designs, Zella wondered how Michael would feel about seeing his ex-wife.

Speaking of ex's, Clive Berry was in Chesterfield opening up a new branch of *Sapphires* when he bumped to Patsy

"Hello, Clive."

"Well hello, Patsy… How are you? And how's married life, of course."

"Oh fine… you know."

"I'm glad to hear it."

"I'm so sorry you and Zella broke up."

"It was bound to happen seeing as she was in love with another man."

Patsy looked confused and asked him what he was talking about, she didn't understand.

"She was in love with someone else, did she never tell you?"

"Who was she in love with?"

"Well he… No, better not, it'd just look like I'm jealous. You must ask her about the love of her life. It's been nice seeing you Patsy… Bye."

"Clive, you must tell me who my sister is in love with… Do I know him?"

"I think you just might."

Patsy waited with baited breath for Clive had to tell her who this man was but he insisted she should ask her sister. He had lit the fuse just enough to start the fire to intrigue Patsy. She would now desperately want to find out about this man her sister was in love with.

"Clive wait… you *must* tell me who this was."

"You ask Zella."

Meanwhile Alden was still in Milan and he was sat in the hotel bar drowning his sorrows staring into an half empty glass when a sudden movement alerted him to that fact Marlene May was standing next to him. He hadn't even noticed her, he was so deep in thought, just minding his own business

"Could I have a glass of champagne?"

"Yes of course , Miss May."

While she waited for her drink she glanced to the side of her then took a good look at Alden.

"Has anyone ever told you that you look like Alvin Preston?"

Alden looked up from his glass. "Miss May?"

"Well...? Have they...?: She insisted.

"I suppose so... a few people have said that."

"You're Alden Pearce aren't you? The reporter interviewing me tomorrow?"

"Yep... that's me."

"Would you care to join me?"

"Yeah... why not."

"Don't put yourself out on my account."

"I won't."

Marlene was quite taken with Alden's attitude. He said what he meant. He didn't mince his words, he just came out with it. She was used to men falling at her feet, letting her have whatever she wanted and telling her what she wanted to hear. Alden was not that kind of man. He'd had enough of women telling him lies and letting them walk all over him.

"Whatever we talk about tonight is off the record."

"Yes, of course. I'm not working now, am I?"

"I thought reporters were always working... looking for that big story"

"Yeah well… not tonight I'm not."

"You looked as if you were miles away when I came to the bar."

"I was…"

"Lady trouble?"

Alden laughed. "Always lady trouble."

Marlene moved closer to him and whispered in his ear, "Who's the lady? Your wife, somebody else's wife or lover… or maybe *both*?" She smirked mischievously.

"Ha…ha. You're cute."

"It has been said." She said confidently.

She reached over and took his hand.

"Shall we take this to my room?" She suggested, seductively.

Alden's eyes lit up and he nodded eagerly. They made their way to the lift passing Derick on the way. He turned, his mouth dropping to the floor as he watched Alden get in the lift with one of his all-time favourite women. Alden winked as the doors closed.

As they entered her suite, she hardly gave him time to get in before she pressed against him, her fingers unzipping his trousers. Moving her hand to his manhood she gripped it, easing her hand over it making him very horny and very stiff. Not requiring much persuasion, he ripped her dress in the rush to get it off. Swiftly, he spun her around, pressing her against the wall. Her dressed pooled round her feet and she quickly kicked it away. His hands swirled all over her creamy, silky body. Gasping, he pulled her panties down and entered her from behind.

"Ahhhh…" She moaned loudly.

"Oh yessss baby... That's it, move onto me... Ohhhh yeah, feel me..."

The more he talked dirty to her the more she groaned and responded. They were like two wild animals puffing and panting, hot and sticky. She pulled him to the bed, her mouth pleasing him as his eyes rolled to the back of his head. *'No, No!'* he thought, *'I can't come yet.'* He pulled on her hips to change her position and she moaned again and again. Holding her breasts he kept his pace steady. Her body tingled, the pleasure was electric and fast, she trembled at his touch. Their lovemaking went on for some considerable time Finally, Alden couldn't hold on any longer and emptied himself into her. They collapsed on the bed, smiling at each other, both completely satisfied, before they drifted off into sleep. The next morning Marlene nudged Alden awake.

"Wake up, darling. We need to get a move on."

"Ahhhh... really? What time is it?" He opened his sleepy eyes and pushed his hair into shape with his fingers.

"Time you were up. Are you coming to the press conference?"

"What press conference?"

"With Matt Adams, Vivian Towers, Elaine Crystal, Millicent Lee and myself ....We are funding the London Fashion Show for charity."

Alden informed her that he hadn't been invited, she told him that he just had been. He was thrilled. He jumped up and got dressed giving Marlene a kiss on the cheek as he left. He dashed to his room, had a quick wash and threw on a fresh shirt. He grabbed Derick and headed for the conference room.

"You can't come in here… just invited reporters." The security man stated.

"I'm a reporter and this is my cameraman."

"Who invited you?"

"Me…" Marlene's voice came from behind.

"I'm so sorry. Miss May."

As she walked in she grabbed Alden's hand, leading the way.

"Thanks for that, Marlene."

"Darling, after last night you can have anything you please." She said, winking at him.

Derick looked at Alden inquisitively. Alden smiled which quickly turned into a smug smirk. Just at that moment Matt Adams walks in with Vivian Towers Elaine Crystal and Millicent Lee. Matt had just broken through in the film industry with his first major movie.

Flash bulbs were exploding in all directions, after all Matt had four beautiful women by his side. Every reporter in the room, including Alden, wanted shots of Vivian Towers in particular. She had been voted one of most beautiful woman in the world, with her shoulder length, raven black hair, violet eyes and sultry looks. She oozed sex appeal and rumour had it that Matt Adams had fallen head over heels and was set to marry her.

"Vivian, what's it like to be in a Matt Adams production?"

"He's strict and he makes you work." She laughed.

Milly nodded her head, smiling, "Yes, if you want a part in a Matt Adams film you have to earn it." She giggled.

175

"You have to be word perfect." Vivian chuckled, Elaine agreed by nodding her head vigorously, choking back her laughter.

"Are you and Matt getting married?" A reporter shouted out.

"Matt, you can answer that one!" Vivian smiled.

"Hmmm... You will have to wait and see."

Marlene's eyes rested on Alden.

"Marlene... what is the charity in aid of?" He shouted to her

"Well, Mr Pearce, we want to raise money for a new wing to be built in the London hospital for terminally ill patients."

"That's very commendable"

"Thank you."

"Elaine... is there a new film in the pipeline?" A reporter from the back shouted

"Well, my sugar dumpling... yes there is."

The press fired question after question until Matt stood up and told them that was all for the minute,

"You've got your story, guys."

The press surrounded Vivian just for the photos – she was just so beautiful and knew how to work the camera. Matt led Vivian Elaine and Millicent out while Marlene made her way over to Alden.

"When do you want to interview me, Mr Pearce?"

"Now would be good..."

"Shall we go to the garden? It would be the perfect place, it's so pretty."

They were about to make their way to the garden when Matt shouted to Alden.

"Yes, Mr Adams?"

"How would you and your camera man like an exclusive?"

"I would love that Mr Adams."

Matt handed him a card. "Call me and we'll set it up."

"Wow thank you. Can I ask *why me*?"

"I like you… and you were the only one who asked about the charity."

Alden rushed off to his interview with Marlene. She wasn't amused, she didn't like being kept waiting, but seeing it was Alden she let it go and led him outside. She was right about the garden, it was very pretty. They went through the door to an arch that took them to a gravel path leading to four benches round an ornate fountain with water lillies floating on the surface. The whole garden was surrounded by big English elm trees. You could smell the beautiful aroma coming from them and the fresh flowers. Derick set up his equipment while Marlene freshened up her make up.

"Ready when you are, Al."

"OK… Marlene, are you ready?"

"Yes…"

Derick held up his finger to indicate his count down.
"OK… 3-2-1 Action! Camera's rolling."

"Thank you so much Miss May, for letting me interview you."

"My pleasure, darling."

"What made you want to a model?"

"Well, I thought I would be good at it." She giggled confidently.

"You weren't the only one that thought you had a bright future in modelling, were you?"

"Michael Charles said I was perfect for modelling."

"He was right... you are simply beautiful."

"Ohhhhh Thank you, darling."

"Do you get to keep the clothes you model?"

"Yes... some of them."

"What do you think of Zella Russell's designs?"

"I like them... they're different and fresh."

He went on to ask her what she was working on next and she informed him that, alongside Matt, Vivian, Elaine and Millicent she would be concentrating on raising funds for the new hospital wing in London. Their interview drew to a close.

"Thank you, Miss May. Its been a real pleasure."

"The pleasure was all mine, darling." She winked at him.

Chapter 23

When Zella and Michael got back to London, Michael just had to finish his photoshoot the next morning, then he was all hers. She told him she had already made arrangements to see her mum so she was going home for a few days

"Not to worry, I'll do the photoshoots tomorrow. Now here's an idea, why don't I meet you in Chesterfield?"

"You want to come to Chesterfield? My mother is gonna wanna meet you!"

"Yes… that's good. I want to meet her and spend the few days we have off with you."

"OK… that would be great."

Michael finished his two day photoshoots then made his way to Zella in Chesterfield. Carlos knew she was going home to see her mum and had asked her if she would kindly look in on the Chesterfield branch. He told her he suspected that some materials were disappearing. Large orders for materials were being placed and the money was being taken from the account but the stock was still low. He suspected the branch manager was behind it. Zella told him she would visit but not tell them she was going in to check the books.

"You need a really good manager in there."

"Yes I know, but who? You are the only person I know from there, do you know of anybody who would want the manager's job"

"Yes I do, actually. She would be perfect to run the factory."

"Who...?"

"Peggy Health, she was my manager before I worked for you."

"OK, let's find out what going on and, if what I suspect is right, then the job is hers."

Carlos trusted Zella with anything and everything. He knew she would find out what was going.

When she arrived back in Chesterfield she went straight home to see her mum. Florence was so pleased to see her. She asked how long she had her home for Zella said a few day and there is someone I would like you to meet. Florence asked if she had a new beau.

"That's so lovely, mum."

"What...?

"*Beau*"

"You know what I mean..."

Zella leaned in to kiss her mother and giggled at the same time, "Yes, a new beau." They sat down with a cup of tea and had a chat. Zella mentioned that she had to pop out to see what was going on in the factory. Florence was really impressed that her daughter's boss had so much faith and trust in her. As it turned out, Zella caught Roger red handed and he had no chance of denying what he had been up to and left immediately. Zella called Carlos to let him know and he told her to ask her friend if she wanted the job.

The next morning Zella caught the bus to the boutique. She looked in the window and there was Peggy, pottering about. As soon as Zella walked in she grinned from ear to ear.

"Hello Darling, please say you want your job back, I have missed having you around the place."

"No... but I do have a proposition for you."

Peggy looked intrigued, "Please tell."

Zella explained everything that had happened. Peggy was immediately interested in the job, especially when Zella told her it came with perks like more money and she could take some Zella Russell brands home with her.

"*Done*... You convinced me."

"You'll take the job?"

"Yesssssssssss...."

"Excellent... Carlos will be so pleased."

"Carlos?"

"Our boss"

Zella called Carlos to tell him the good news and to let him know Peggy couldn't start until the following week. He told that was fine and said he would be there to greet her on her first day to go over her contract. He asked if Zella would mind keeping an eye on everything while she was home. She reassured him she would keep her eyes on the factory.

Michael checked into his hotel. He couldn't wait to meet up with Zella, he had missed her. He realised he had fallen for her which was rare since, after Marlene, he didn't get in too deep. Marlene had stung him and he was still wary. As for Zella, she loved catching up with her mum, it was so nice being home. A bit later on Patsy came round and, while Florence was busy preparing afternoon tea, she and Zella caught up

"Zella…? Can I ask you something?"

"Of course."

"Have you ever done anything you know you shouldn't, but you did it anyway?"

"I em… I suppose I have, I don't know. Why?"

"I have…"

"What?"

Patsy suddenly shut up, "Oh it's nothing."

"It can't be that bad can it? Come on Patsy, what did you do?"

Patsy shrugged her shoulders, "Nothin… forget it."

Zella looked at her side-eyed. What an odd think to ask, Zella thought.

Then Patsy blurted out, "Who is the man you fell in love with?"

"What do you mean?"

"Your marriage failed because of this man… Who is he?"

Zella looked at Patsy, horrified. "What are you talking about?"

"Clive told me"

"When did you see Clive?"

"Oh… a week or so ago."

"Clive was jealous and manipulative. He thought I was seeing someone else."

"And were you?"

"Of course not."

"He sounded very sure."

"Clive had been paranoid the whole of our marriage. He was jealous over every man I spoke to. "

"So there was no other man?"

"No…"

"Soooooo… Michael… is this love?"

"I don't know… you'll like him… so will mum."

"It sounds like love."

Zella smiled as a warm feeling swept into her heart as she said his name. Whilst Patsy and Florence made afternoon tea, she went off to meet Michael. He told her he was looking forward to meeting her mother and sister.

Florence had been busy all morning making cakes and sandwiches, she had even made cookies. She had really gone to town, she was so looking forward to meeting Michael, she hoped he would be an improvement on Clive.

Patsy was first at the door, "Hello Michael."

"Well, hello Patsy." He paused for a moment, "You *are* Patsy?"

"Yes…"

"Phew!" He said, brushing his hair back.

She stood there staring at him with her mouth open, '*Oh My God, he's Gorgeous!*' She thought to herself.

Florence sauntered out of the kitchen trying desperately not to look too eager.

"Hello Michael, it's nice to meet you." She held her hand out to him.

"The pleasure is all mine, Mrs Russell. I can see where Zella gets her beauty."

Florence was flattered and blushed a little, she was won over instantly. Zella smirked thinking what a smooth talker he was, he had Patsy and Florence eating out of the palm of his hand. Zella and Patsy went to get the tea leaving Florence with Michael chatting.

When they came back Florence was smiling and laughing at his humour. He had certainly made a first good impression.

"Please help yourself to afternoon tea, Michael." Florence smiled. Zella was taken back by her mother, she was positively gushing.

Alden finally made a late appearance, "Good evening, Michael."

"Have you been working, Alden?"

"Yep, you know what it's like, reporters never rest, a young lady told me that recently... now who was it? OH... yes, it was your ex-wife."

"You've been married, Michael?" Florence asked curiously.

"Yes... to the model Marlene May."

"Marlene May!" Patsy gasped.

"It didn't work out."

Florence asked him about his work and how he started and whether he enjoyed his job.

"I work long hours and travel. I love my job and that's how I met Zella. I have been seeing Zella for a while now and I can safely say I'm in love with your daughter, Mrs Russell."

Zella looked straight at Michael. She was most certainly shocked at what he'd just said. Alden was also shocked but couldn't take it in, he didn't want to hear that. As a result, bile and sarcasm spilled from his mouth all evening. Patsy couldn't understand how rude he was being. Florence Zella and Patsy cleared up and while they were in the kitchen, Michael asked Alden what his problem was.

"I don't have a problem."

"Oh… I think you do."

Alden sat cockily back on his chair and matter of factly said, "Nope."

"You think I'm not good enough for Zella…"

"You're *not*…"

Michael nodded his head, "I see… Maybe you are… I think I know what your problem is."

"You know *shit*."

Alden was moody all evening, a fact that was becoming more noticeable to everyone as the evening went on. When they arrived home, Patsy shouted at Alden, "You were really embarrassing and very rude."

"So…"

"Why…?"

He glared at her with angry eyes. She told him she was going to bed as she'd had enough of him for one night. A few minutes later he appeared at the bedroom door.

"Take your nightdress off"

185

She sat up wondering if she was hearing him right. He was demanding, masterful, she found it very arousing. She watched him take his clothes off and then slide in next to her.

"This is what you want, isn't it?"

Patsy eagerly took her nightdress off, throwing it across the room. In one swift moment his hands were all over her. He held her hips firmly as moved himself between her thighs. She sighed with excitement as he pushed his erection towards her, thrusting into her, back and forth in rhythm. Her body shuddered every time he touched her. He toyed with her breasts making her nipples stand to attention, she felt dizzy with the excitement. His rhythm got faster then he climaxed before rolling off her and turning away from her. 'This must be a good sign,' she thought. She felt good the next morning and made her husband breakfast. She felt as if she had made a breakthrough.

"Good morning." She said, placing egg, bacon and toast in front of him

"What are you doing?"

"Breakfast for my husband."

"Look Patsy, last night was just sex nothing more. I wanted it, you gave it."

Patsy lip began to quiver, her eyes beginning to fill with tears.

"There you go again, reading more into things than there are. You don't listen – I'm in love with someone I can't have because of your lies. I cheat on you, why don't you divorce me?"

"I *love* you. I think we could have a good life together if you would just give it a chance."

"You *think* you're in love with me. I was honest with you, I told you I didn't love you. You should be with a man who loves you."

"I want that man to be *you.*"

Alden sighed heavily, "You don't fucking listen."

He grabbed his jacket and stormed out, slamming the door. He was so stressed when he got to the office that Derick asked him what was wrong.

"That fuckin' woman…"

"Patsy…?"

"Yep…"

"What's happened?"

"I told her I cheat on her… I told her to divorce me… but, Oh no…"

"You told her you cheat on her? And she still wants you? Wow, that's my kinda woman!" He laughed.

"It's not fuckin' funny, Derick."

Derick held his hands up. He suggested to Alden that he tell Patsy who the woman he wanted was.

"If you have no better suggestions, don't say another word."

"It was just a thought."

"Well, think again."

Derick knew Alden wasn't happy with Patsy. He had never seen Alden so unhappy and he also knew it would end badly when the truth finally came out. He sat back on his chair and Bessie suddenly came into his mind. He missed her and decided to go visit her in his dinner hour. He sat himself down on the grass beside her grave and spoke to her as if she was right there beside him. He took her picture out of his wallet, the picture he looked at every day.

"I miss you, Bessie." And he began told her all his news and all about Alden.

A lady was stood not so far from him. She must have been visiting someone as well and she smiled as she overheard him.

"Was this your girl?"

"Yes, she was taken from me very suddenly we were going to get married."

"I'm so sorry.

"Is that your husband?"

"Yes he was taken from me suddenly, too."

"I'm sorry."

He turns his head to see who he was talking to and lo and behold there stood Glenda.

"Hello, Derick."

"Glenda, how are you?"

"I'm alright. I still feel dreadful about Bessie."

"Why?"

"I was the one who arranged the abortion."

"You were, but that man needs to be reported."

"I don't know who he is."

"But you arranged it!"

"Through someone else..."

Derick's heart was heavy as he stood up and said good bye to Bessie, telling he loved her and would always love her. He made his way back to work but he couldn't concentrate. Bessie stayed in his thoughts all day.

Chapter 24

Back in London, Vivian Towers had gone to see Dorian to ask for recommendations for a designer for her wedding dress. His first response was to ask why she wasn't asking *him*.

"I know you are busy with fashion shows."

"Yes, very true. Well I do know a designer, her name is Zella… Zella Russell"

"I've heard that name before."

"Yes… she's very talented"

"Have you a number for her?"

Dorian passed Zella's card over to Vivian and told her to give Zella call.

"I will. Thanks, Dorian."

"You'll be impressed with Zella, you'll like her."

The following morning, Viv called Zella to set up a meeting. Zella was overflowing with excitement, the one and only Vivian Towers was asking *her* to make her wedding dress. Was she dreaming? She certainly felt she was, she even had to pinch herself to make sure.

Next day, Zella made her way to her meeting with Miss Towers to discuss the design and whether or not Zella could make the dress in time.

"Well, what do you think, Zella?"

"Yes, Miss Towers, we can make this dress in time for your wedding."

"Marvellous, not a word to Matt though!" Vivian giggled.

Zella got to work straight away. She picked the best silk she could find and a romantic lace for the lace quarter length sleeves Vivian had insisted on.

Not too long after, she called Vivian for her first fitting. Zella sat talking to Vivian's friend Millicent Lee while they waited for her to come out of the changing room. Vivian had a beautiful hour glass figure and Zella and Millicent both gasped as she stepped out to revel the dress,

"Oh my, you are so beautiful."

"Thank you."

It was just a little big on Vivian so Zella started making some adjustments.

"What do you think, Milly?"

"You're simply stunning darling. You are going to knock Matt's socks off."

Zella gave a little giggle and Vivian smiled.

"A little bird tells me that you are seeing the handsome Michael Charles."

"Well…"

"Come on darling, spill the beans." Milly said excitedly and winked. "I do love a little gossip."

"I have been seeing Michael, yes."

"You see, Marlene was right." Milly said, her eyes widened with excitement.

"Oh, his ex-wife told you?"

"Yes… That gorgeous reporter told her, apparently while they were between the sheets." She laughed heartily.

"Do you mean Alden Pearce?"

Vivian nudged Milly discreetly when she saw the look on Zella's face.

"No, no… I don't think that was his name, Zella."

Milly looked hesitantly at Vivian , making the *'what have I said'* face.

"I should hope not. He's my brother in law."

"Oh really… I'm not sure who Alden is darling, maybe I have mixed him up with someone else" Milly said, still looking at Vivian.

Zella changed the subject by asking Vivian to come in the following week for another fitting.

When Vivian and Milly got out side Milly said, "Oh shit…" placing her hand on top of her head

"You are my best friend and I can say this… you have the biggest mouth. You will get someone divorced one day."

"Oops…" She giggled mischievously.

Meanwhile Alden was back in Chesterfield when he got a call from Matt Adams asking him when he wanted to do his exclusive interview.

"Whenever you are ready, Mr Adams."

"Well, what about tomorrow?"

"Sure… where, what time?"

"Well, I'm in Brighton, can you and your camera man get there for 10am?"

"Yes, we'll be there."

He rushed round to Derick's.

"Pack a bag, we're off to Brighton!"

"Brighton…?"

"Yep, my friend, we have an exclusive with Mr Matt Adams."

"You're shitting me!"

They headed to the train station and caught the train to Brighton, checking in to Drakes Inn not far from hotel where Matt was staying, overlooking the seafront. They walked along the beachfront and headed to the nearest café for something to eat and then spent a couple of hours sat in the pub.

Alden's interview with Matt Adams

The next morning after breakfast they went to meet Matt at his hotel. Derick set his equipment up while Alden chatted to Matt. Matt had arranged a plush room for the interview and they took their seats in two deep green velvet chairs. Derick informed them that he was ready to roll when they were and they both nodded.

"Hello Matt, really nice to meet you and thank you for taking the time to give me an exclusive. I know you are a busy man."

"Hello Alden."

"Let me start by congratulating you on your charity work – for the new wing at the London hospital."

"Thanks, it's been fantastic… and all the donations have been amazing."

"That's outstanding. I'm so pleased. Now, can I ask you what inspired you to want to make films?"

"Well I was always interested in photos and how I could make them move. My grandfather left me a camera when I was about twelve and my long-time friend Jake Summers, well his parents scraped up enough money to get him one too and we would bet each other which one of could get the most interesting photos."

Alden smiled, "Who won?"

"We both did, really."

"So how did you actually get into the business?"

"I got a job sweeping a studio floor then I progressed to making the tea." He laughed. "Then I was given a lucky break by my old friend Bruce Anderson, he took me under his wing and taught me everything I know."

"So tell me, what do you think makes a good film?"

"Something that grips you, keeps you on the edge of your seat, if you have a great script you get a great film"

"Who is your dream artist?"

"Oh my, that's a good question, there are so many… Maryanne Morton, Tony Walters, Lena Thomson, Ramona Hammond and, of course, Vivian Towers."

Alden nodded in agreement, thinking that it was a nice touch adding Vivian in like that.

"What areas would you like to explore in the future?"

"Hmm, bigger, better films, I'm open to any challenge."

"Thank you so much, Matt."

"My pleasure…"

"Just one more question… are you and Vivian set to marry?"

"Yes… our wedding date has been set and she has a designer making her dress as we speak."

"I wish you both every happiness for the future."

Clapping his hands together, Derick shouted, "That's it, guys! It's a wrap."

Chapter 25

Michael had asked Zella to go to Austria with him and some others. A friend owned a log cabin resort and he had offered Michael two cabins. Zella jumped at the chance, she had never been to Austria before. What she hadn't realised was that Michael had asked Patsy and Alden too. When Patsy told her she and Alden would be going with them she didn't know whether to laugh or cry, even though it would be good to have a holiday with her sister

When they arrived at the hotel they could see why it had been called the *Grand View Resort*. It was all of that, a grand view of the mountain, the lake and the surrounding trees, it was magnificent. When they went inside Patsy couldn't believe her eyes. It had a massive chimney breast in the centre of the room, three sets of steps led to the bar, lounge and dining room. Even the bedrooms had sensational views of the glistening snowy mountain tops whichever direction you were facing.

They settled in for a quiet first night. After a meal in the hotel dining room they sat in the bar for the rest of the evening. Bright and early next morning they sat down to breakfast. Zella wanted to try an Austrian breakfast and helped herself to boiled egg cheese, ham and toast followed by a croissant with butter and honey washed down with a pot of coffee.

"Were you hungry?" Michael asked.

"Yes, I was ravenous, that was lovely."

"Are you all ready for skiing?"

"I can't ski."

"I'll show you."

Patsy interrupted, "I'm ready."

"You don't ski either," Zella smiled.

"No… but I'm ready to learn"

Alden said he skied a little and so they headed to the slopes. Michael took them to the gentle slopes for beginners and they caught the cable car to the top. As it happened, Patsy took to it like a duck to water. She and Michael soon disappeared from sight, leaving Alden and Zella behind.

Unfortunately there was a storm brewing and Alden and Zella got a little lost. Patsy and Michael had got back to find that they were not there and went back to look for them. The storm was getting stronger when Michael suggested they go back and inform the ski patrol. Patsy was starting to get worried but Michael reassured her that they would be alright.

Meanwhile, Zella had ploughed into a big mountain of snow, twisting her ankle so it was taking her all her time just to keep up with Alden. He slowed down to make sure she was still with him and saw she was struggling with her ankle. It had swollen right up, making it harder to move so he suggested that they rest a while.

"I don't think that's a good idea. The storm is getting worse and we need to get back."

They carried on but the snow was getting heavier until they could hardly see. Alden took his belt from his ski pants and tied it round Zella's wrist so he wouldn't lose her. Just ahead, the path led to a drift that looked like it had been carved into the shape of a cave. He thought they would be able to shelter there for a while, although the fog was getting thicker. The snow was coming down faster, they could barely see anything.

"We are getting nowhere, Zella. Let's wait here for a while to see if the storm passes."

Zella nodded in agreement. She hobbled into the shelter and they settled down to wait. It started getting darker and colder. Alden put his arms around Zella, explaining they needed to keep warm she agreed.

As he held her tight she felt safe and warm. Sharing their body heat would keep them both from freezing to death.

"Do you remember when we use to do this in the car?"

"Yes... that was a long time ago when things were very different."

She felt his cheek next to hers. They were so close. She had to control her feelings, his breath on her cheek took her back to happier days. It would have been very easy to tell him she loved him.

The storm didn't let up and they huddled together, eventually falling asleep enveloped in each other's arms. When they eventually woke up they were hungry, cold and wet. Fortunately the storm had now passed so all they had to do was find their way back. That wouldn't be easy either as Zella's ankle was the size of a balloon. Luckily, before they got too far, the rescue team found them and the paramedics took care of her foot before taking them back to the hotel where Patsy and Michael were waiting. They were so pleased to see them back safe.

"Zella, Alden! Oh my!" Patsy shouted and flung her arms round them both.

"We're alright." Alden muttered.

Michael took hold of Zella and kissed her, "I was so worried about you."

Zella smiled, "We need to get out of these wet clothes and get warm and then find something to eat."

Alden smiled at Zella and she smiled warmly back at him.

It was safe to say Zella didn't want to go skiing for the rest of the holiday. She was able to find some local shops that she could hobble round, doing a little retail therapy. She and Patsy found two shops, Ararinda and Gabriele's, that sold lots of the latest designs. They even found a Zella Russell design .

"Zella look, it's one of your designs."

Zella giggled happily "Wow, that's exciting!"

The sales assistant greeted them. "Guten Morgen"

"Guten Morgen Zella smiled.

The young woman showed them some of the new designs they had just got in, even showing them some of Zella own designs. There was a whole rack of her dresses. The young lady had no idea who Zella was, she just carried on showing them round.

198

They had been walking round for an hour or so when Zella told Patsy she needed to finish, her foot was throbbing and needed rest so they went over to a little café on the corner.

"Guten Morgen."

"Guten Morgen. Could I please order two coffees, hmm *Mélange*."

The man smiled. "Two mélanges."

She also ordered two sandwiches that looked something like an omelette in a croissant with cheese and ham and then two slices of apfelstrudel. They were so ready for this after their exertions in the shops and enjoyed every bit of it. They sat and talked for a while before having another coffee.

"Alden cheats on me..." Patsy suddenly blurted out.

"No... Patsy you're wrong."

"No...no ... he told me. Remember when I met him?"

Zella nodded, unsure what was coming next.

"He was seeing someone," Patsy confessed.

"That doesn't mean he's seeing her now."

"No he's not, just everyone else."

"I think you're wrong."

Patsy shook her head in disagreement, "You're lucky Michael wants you, he's going to ask you to marry him."

"I don't want to get married again. I like the way things are"

"Why... Was Clive so bad that he put you off?"

"I just want to concentrate on my career."

As they walked back slowly back to the hotel Patsy asks Zella if she wanted children. "One day," she replied. Patsy confessed she wanted a man who really loved her to settle down and have his children but she felt that wasn't going to be with Alden. She had hoped he would love her like she loved him but it wasn't meant to be she admitted sadly.

As they approached the hotel, Michael and Alden were outside waiting. Michael asked if they'd had a good day. Patsy laughed and said they'd had real sister day. Zella said she was going up to the room to pack and made her way upstairs. She had gone very quiet at dinner and this lasted until the flight home.

When they got back to London, Michael asked Zella if she was staying over but she said she was going back to her flat as she was shattered from the flight home

"Are you alright?"

"Yes…"

She had been thinking about Alden and when they had been stranded in the snowstorm, she hadn't been able to get it off her mind. She knew that she did still love him but she couldn't allow herself to feel like that because he was her sister's husband. She also thought about Patsy, what she had said about Alden cheating on her and Michael wanting to marry her. Her mind just kept racing over and over the same things.

Chapter 26

The next evening she went to a function with Carlos, a charity do in aid of the new wing at the hospital. Also attending was Matt Adams. Zella and Carlos had been there about an hour when she went over to the bar to get herself a drink. Matt turned to her and stared for a few moments.

"Aren't you Zella Russell?"

"Yes… I am, Mr Adams."

"Please, call me Matt."

Zella smiled softly at him.

"Tell me why women are so complicated."

Zella giggled. "That, Mr Adams, is the million dollar question!"

He smiled, "*Matt* – you make me sound like my father calling me 'Mr Adams'. I'll give **you** a million dollars if you can give me the answer about women. After all ,you are one."

"Yes, some women are more complicated than others."
She smiled

"Let me get you a drink and then you can tell me all
about women."

"Aren't you all set to marry the beautiful Vivian Towers?
I have worked very hard on her dress, you know."

"Tell me, Zella, have you ever been in love?"

"Ohhhh yes, he broke my heart into a million pieces."

"Well, I am in love, and someone has kindly told her that
I've cheated on her… So there may well not be a
wedding at all."

"Have you…?"

"No…"

"Then there *will* be a wedding. Because if she didn't love
you anymore she wouldn't be so upset would she?"

"This man that broke your heart needs his head testing
because you are lovely lady, intelligent and beautiful
and he doesn't deserve your love."

"It up to you to make Vivian see sense. Make her see how
much you love her and that you don't need anyone
else."

He smiled at gently, taking her hand and kissing it softly.
He thanked her for the chat and he would certainly be
taking her advice.

A couple of days later Michael asked Zella out to dinner.
She was still a little quiet with him. He sat opposite her and
stared at her, studying her face. He had always loved the
way she bit her lip when she was listening to him speak,
the way her eyes sparkled when she was excited about
something and, of course, that beautiful smile. However, he

hadn't seen any of this for the past few days. He knew there was something on her mind. He reached over the table and took her hand.

"I love you Zella"

She smiled warmly at him.

"I have something I want to ask you"

She tried to change the subject by talking about the new photoshoot he had planned.

"Zella…"

"Please don't, Michael."

"You don't know what I was going to ask you."

"I think I do."

"Marry me…"

"I can't…"

"Has this got something to do with Alden?"

"Michael…?"

"It has…hasn't it?" He interrupted her. "You love him don't you?"

"I don't know what you mean."

"I think you do, I've seen the way you look at him and more to the point the way he looks at you. He's the one you've always loved, isn't he?"

She lowered her head and finally admitted how she felt about Alden. "I've always loved him."

"I knew it… I'll get you a taxi. I think we have finished here."

She wanted to explain but he wouldn't give her the chance. He put her in the taxi and told her he really didn't want to hear it. She begged him to listen but he wouldn't. He watched the taxi drive away then, making his way to the river, he sat on a bench thinking how stupid he was for thinking she could fall in love with him, again he had given his heart only to have it broken.

In work the next morning, Carlos walked into her office to say hello and she burst into tears. He sat down and tried to make sense of what she was telling him. He was so good with her, he was the closest thing to a father figure she had, he sat for hours while she told him the whole story complete with stutters and splutters. He waited a few seconds after she had sobbed herself to a halt and suggested that she should do what makes her happy.

He was curious as to why she didn't tell Patsy that Alden was her man.

"I wasn't going to hurt Patsy"

"But she's hurt you. OK, she doesn't know she hurt you but she *has*."

"When Michael asked me to marry him last night, my heart dropped. I couldn't say yes. I married Clive and that was a disaster, I should never have let that happen."

"What are you going to do? Because the way I see it you will never be happy until you admit to Alden that you still love him."

"I can't *ever* do that."

"Zella…"

He took her hands and told her she's a beautiful women and she should be happy. Carlos was very fond of Zella and he was worried about her.

"I never wanted to hurt Michael."

"I know…"

Chapter 27

Vivian called Zella at the office as she wanted to meet up with her about one last fitting for her wedding dress.

"Hi, Zella."

"Hello, Miss Towers. Are you ready for your big day?"

"That why I called, will you meet me for lunch at my suite. I seem to have lost a little weight…"

"And you want me to make some alterations?"

"Only if you think it needs it."

"OK, I'd love to."

"Thanks."

That afternoon Zella made her way to the hotel and up to Vivian's suite. As she moved her arm forward to knock on the door, Vivian opened it.

"Ohhhh! Hello, Miss Towers."

"Oh please, call me Viv."

"Let's have a look at this dress."

Vivian went into the bedroom and reappeared in her wedding dress.

"You really are going to be a stunning bride on Saturday."

"Thanks to you… I love this dress. Do you think Matt will like it?"

"He'd be mad not to. But it's you who make the dress, it's all you."

"You are so kind."

"It's true, you are so beautiful. Now let's have a look, and turn for me."

As Vivian turned Zella made a few marks. It only need a few little adjustments, nothing drastic. She didn't even need to take it away, she made the adjustments right there. Vivian was soon all ready for the big day. She insisted Zella stay for lunch and they chatted. Pouring a glass of wine, Vivian asked about Michael and did she think he would pop the question. Zella told her that she and Michael had called it a day.

"Oh, I'm sorry to hear that."

"Don't be, it was sort of my doing."

"Oh, I see…"

"Well, I didn't want to hurt him. I know that Miss May did."

"But why would you think you'd hurt him?"

"Because I'm in love with someone else."

"Oh, Zella…"

"It's alright."

"I want you come to the wedding. Please say you'll come."

"I would love to and thank you for lunch, but unfortunately I've got to go."

"Yes, of course. See you Saturday – your name will be on the guest list."

"Thank you so much."

Saturday: Vivian and Matt's big day

When Zella arrived at the Silver Bridge Hotel, she felt a little out of place. She'd never attended anything on her own before, never mind a big lavish wedding such as this. Millicent had spotted her and made her way over.

"Hello, Darling."

"Miss Lee, Hello."

"You have made quite an impression on Viv, she really likes you."

"I like her too – she's so nice."

"Who are you with Darling?"

"No one…"

"Fabulous, Darling – me too. We can get through this together."

Zella smiled and thought what an odd thing that was to say, surely it would be *attend* the wedding together? As Vivian walked towards Matt, Zella was admiring the draped lemon white flowers which formed the backdrop to the altar when Millicent muttered, "Do you think she has added a little weight? That dress looks a little tight."

"No… she's lost weight. I had to take the dress in just two days ago."

"Oh right… It just looked… Oh well, never mind."

"She is stunning."

"Hmmm."

Zella thought Millicent was acting a tad odd considering it was her best friend's wedding, odd bordering on pure jealousy. Zella gazed across to the other side only to see Michael with a young lady, the young lady in question being the model Anne Foster. Michael had spotted Zella from afar and planned to go nowhere near her.

After the ceremony Matt and Vivian made their way to the gardens for photographs while their guests were shown to the ballroom where the reception was being held. Elaine spotted Milly and came over. There was no love lost between the two, Elaine blamed Milly for the break up between her and Matt in the 50s.

"Milly, how are you?"

Millicent sighed. "I'm fine."

"Beautiful wedding, they look so happy."

"Hmmm… I don't think it will last though."

"Well…. It won't if *you* have anything to do with it."

"What do you mean by that?"

"Well don't you find its funny how things go wrong when you are around… Ohhhhh, by the way… *I know what you did*."

"What the hell are you talking about?"

Elaine whispered in Milly's ear and the colour suddenly drained from her face,

"Ludicrous…!"

Just then Priscilla interrupted, noticing Milly's grey face, "You alright Milly?"

"Yes I'm fine." She snapped.

"She's just *dandy*… aren't you, Milly?"

"Excuse me a moment…"

208

Millicent quickly departed their company. Priscilla looked at Elaine and asked what she had said to her.

"Nothing… *Much…*" She smirked triumphantly.

"Well… Whatever you said it's certainly ruffled her feathers."

Elaine knew she had Milly on the back foot, she had really spooked her with her revelation.

Meanwhile, on the other side of the room Zella was admiring the setting. Vivian sure had taste, there was a big swing/jazz band on the stage, and every table was decorated in lemon and white. There were some big names in that room. Zella found herself daydreaming, thinking this was a world she could get used to, when a voice beside her said, "Hello…"

She turned her head to the right side of her there sitting next to her was Peter Martin, the American actor. She was a huge fan.

"Oh my!"

"Hello, doll. Where have you been all my life"

"Ummm"

"No… don't say another word. You, Babycakes, are coming with me."

"Where…?"

"You'll see"

Peter took her by the hand and led her over to a table.

"Jake…?"

Jake turned his head in the direction of Peter and looked Zella up and down.

"Wow…" Jakes eyes lit up with excitement.

"Yep, Jake, are you thinking what I'm thinking?"

"Excuse me, but what are you *both* thinking?" Zella asked, totally confused.

Just then, Matt and Vivian returned and Vivian make a point of introducing Zella

"I see you've met my designer, Jake." She could see his eyes had lit up with excitement.

"*Designer*...? She's your designer?"

"Yes, meet Zella Russell – the next big designer."

Peter looked at Vivian. "Ohhhhh..." and took Zella's hand. "We are going to dance now. Come on, doll!"

"I thought I had another top model in the making then." Jake said

Matt laughed. "Always on the lookout for that next big star."

"You win some, you lose some, but she is stunning, though." He laughed playfully. Jake Summer had a good eye for spotting talent.

Zella had the most amazing day, and the most exciting too, as she danced with two Hollywood film stars, one Peter Martin and the other Brad Cannon. She danced the night away and Michael managed to stay away from her although he watched her from afar.

Chapter 28

Months has passed since the wedding and Zella had tried to call Michael but he just wouldn't return any of her calls and simply wouldn't go to any photoshoot that she was to attend. He did, however, have to be at the same fashion show in the Princess Hotel in the middle of London at the weekend, he couldn't get out of it although he had tried. He really wasn't looking forward to seeing her, she had hurt him deeply.

When he arrived, he walked into the bar and there was Marlene.

"Well… Hello, Michael."

"Oh great… just what I need, the ex-wife and the ex-girlfriend in one fell swoop."

"I heard you and Miss Russell were no more. Did she leave you for that gorgeous reporter man?"

"No… Why don't you get back on your fuckin' broom stick and fuck off!"

"Oh my. There's no need to be like that, darling."

"At least she didn't just use me to get what she wanted…"

"Ouch…" He had certainly hit a very raw nerve

"Just go away, Marlene."

He downed his drink in one, leaving Marlene sipping on her champagne. As he went through reception walking toward the lift, he bumped straight into Zella. Giving her a frosty look he pressed the button for the lift.

"Michael… " She shouted

The lift door opened and Alden stepped out. Michael pushed forcefully past him with steam coming out of his ears. Marlene smiled ironically and smirked at Zella, "You really have upset him, haven't you?"

Alden stared, wondering what she could mean.

"I don't know." Zella was close to tears.

Over the passing days she had been watching Alden with the models. It would appear that Patsy had been right. It certainly looked like Alden was cheating on her at every opportunity. She had noticed him getting back into the lift and decided to confront him.

"Wait… hold the door"

She walked into the lift and Alden asked how everything was going with Michael, knowing full well that they had split up'

"I've been watching you." She said, ignoring his question completely.

"Have you… and what did you see?"

"You're messing around with all those models… How dare you treat my sister like that?"

"How dare I…?"

212

He hit the lift button hard and the lift stopped in between floors, making it judder as it ground to a halt. He took hold of Zella's arms and pushed her against the side of the lift, staring intensely into her eyes. He was so close there was no space between them.

"I wish I'd never met your sister, you have no idea what your sister is capable of she has ruined my life"

"What do you mean by that?"

"Maybe it's time you knew the truth about your little sister"

"What do you mean by that? Alden…"

He looked so angry as he told her about how he was going to ask her to marry him but her dear little sister messed all that up. He had just been doing Patsy a favour getting her out of hot water with their mother, "… and then you had run off and married Clive…"

He admitted that he was at fault for sleeping with Patsy, but when she told him she was pregnant, which forced his hand, he had done the honourable thing and married her.

"The only woman I've ever loved is you, Zella. Now back off!"

"You're lying… Patsy wouldn't do that"

"Sorry baby… *but it's all true.*"

Quietly, he pressed the button and the lift started back up. They stood in silence until Alden got out. Zella couldn't believe her sister would do something like that. Why would she?

While Alden was telling Zella some home truths about her sister, Patsy was back home and out on the town with Mary. They were having grand old time with all the new

213

dance crazes, the twist, the locomotion, the mash potato, the swim and the hully gully and even a jive or two. They had been dancing non-stop all evening.

"I need a drink."

"Me too" Mary said, panting. "Look there's Derick!"

"Oh yeah… Come on, let's go over."

They sauntered over and Patsy tapped Derick on the back to make him turn around.

"Hey, Patsy, how's things?"

"What are you doing here? I thought you were in London with Alden."

"Yeah, not this time."

"I thought you were Alden's camera man?"

"I am… he doesn't need a camera man this time. It's just an interview for the paper, so I have a night off."

"Nice…"

"Are you having a good night?"

"Oh yes…"

He smiled and she realised she had never noticed how attractive Derick was.

"Well, are you going to buy me a drink then?"

He laughed, "You're not shy, are you?"

"Nope… no time for that!"

Laughing, he bought her and Mary a drink.

Not only was Patsy pretty, he thought, but forward with it. No wonder she got what she wanted, she knew what she wanted and went for it. Patsy and Mary spent the whole evening with Derick. Mary was developing a bit of a crush on Derick but it was obvious that he liked Patsy.

He even managed to dance with both of them a couple of times and, as the evening drew to a close, he told them he would escort them both home. They dropped Mary off first then made their to Patsy's.

"Are you coming in for a cup of tea?"

"I don't think so, Patsy,"

"Why…?"

"It wouldn't be right – seeing as your Alden's wife and you know what people are like. It would be the talk of the town… in fact, it still could be yet."

"I don't care. The truth is I don't think Alden would either…"

"Why would you say that?" knowing what Alden had already told him in Milan.

"Please come in for a drink?"

"OK… just one cup of tea then."

Patsy put the kettle and asking him if he would like a slice of cake. He nodded and asked if she had made it herself. She smiled and told him that she could do all that stuff, she even joked by saying she'd make someone a good wife one day. Derick found her funny.

She signed heavily as she brewed a pot of tea and cut two slices of Victoria sandwich. They sat down and talked well into the early hours. She told him what she had done to get Alden to marry her and he responded by asking her why she had done it. She shrugged, she wanted him. Trouble was, he didn't want her. By the time Derick left it, was 3am. Had any of her neighbours seen him there would surely be a few rumours. Although he knew she was wrong for tricking Alden, Derick still liked her.

When Alden returned he was soon off again, this time taking Derick with him. They were on their way to Oslo, Norway to cover a story about the new shopping complex they were opening. It was out of this world.

"This place is amazing." Alden enthused.

"Yeah, you can say that again."

"We're going over to Bergen, the west coast of Norway tomorrow."

"That's fantastic… Alden I wanna tell you something'."

"Yeah…? What?"

"I was at your house last week… with Patsy."

"OK…"

"I wanted you to know that's all. Nothing happened…"

"OK… "

"I think I'm in love with Patsy." He blurted out, interrupting him.

"You're in love with her, Derick? Just be careful."

"She told me what she did to get you to marry her."

Alden was shocked. This had always been her way to keep him, and here she was telling Derick the truth. What was she was up to?

"She told you everything? Wow!"

"She's lonely… Alden."

"She can leave…"

"She loves you."

"No, Derick… she just *thinks* she loves me. She needs to realise that's all it is.

"Yeah, maybe

The next day they set off for Bergen to cover the World Archery Championship. Teams from Great Briton, United States, Belgium, and Finland were competing, not to mention South Africa and Czechoslovakia. Alden and Derick both enjoyed the championships, they got loads of material for a great story and Derick captured it all on film. Their boss would be over the moon.

Chapter 29

Patsy called Zella to ask her to come home. Worried, Zella asked what was wrong, why did she need to come home?

"Mum is getting married again."

"What?"

"She is going to call you herself to tell you, but I think you need to come back home for a while."

"Is mum happy?"

"Yes…"

"Well, why do I need to come home?"

"He wants her to move to Devon."

"Oh I see, but mum is entitled to a life of her own… we can always visit."

"Zella, please… just come home."

"OK …OK… I'll talk to Carlos."

When Zella spoke to Carlos to ask if she could work in the Chesterfield branch for a while, he wasn't keen. He didn't want her to leave London but he understood. She told him she would let Dorian and Ingrid know where she was and would carry on her work as normal.

Back in Chesterfield, she went straight to her mum's. When Florence saw her she threw her arms round her, she was so happy to see her.

"So, who's getting married then?"

"Patsy called didn't she? I told her I wanted to tell you myself."

"Congratulations anyway! Where is this lucky man?"

"I'll get Harold to come round."

"I can't wait to meet him."

Harold was duly invited round to meet Zella. When he saw her he commented how beautiful she was. Zella liked him immediately, he was so charming and she could see how much he loved her mother and how happy her mother was.

She was delighted for them both and suggested to Patsy that she give Harold a chance since their mother was happy. Florence had been on her own for a long time and had always put her girls first, it was time for her to think of herself for a change, Patsy conceded that Harold did make Florence happy, she just didn't want them to move away.

Over the weeks Florence and Harold prepared for their big day and Zella jokingly asked if she better look for somewhere to live.

"Why's that, love?"

"Well, you'll be selling this house won't you?"

"I see Patsy has left nothing out."

"No..." Zella giggled.

"When do have to you go back to London?"

"Well, I don't know if I *am* going back yet."

"You can stay here until you make your mind up and if you don't go back you can live here"

"Harold wouldn't mind?"

"No...!"

Before accepting, Zella suggested she should ask him first. As it happened Harold didn't mind at all as he had his own house in Devon. In fact, that's how they had met, when a friend of Florence's had invited her to have a break there. She met Harold in the pub down there and things progressed. He had actually been coming up to see Florence for quite some time, she just hadn't known how to tell Zella and Patsy.

The big day arrived and Florence looked so elegant in her wedding outfit while Harold also looked very dapper in his suit. As he watched his bride walking toward him he smiled, bursting with proud. They had chosen to have just a small reception at the social club and danced the night away, blissfully happy. Next morning, they jumped into the van loaded with Florence's things and tearfully waved goodbye to her girls. It had been a long time that she had shared her life with anyone but her girls and she was ready now to share her life with a man again.

Three days later, out of the blue, Michael turned up. The shock was written all over Zella's face when she answered the door. She wondered why he should come to see her. He had not answered any of her calls, he didn't even speak to her at Matt and Vivian's wedding.

"Michael...?"

"Why did you leave?"

"I needed to come home for a while... please, come in."

220

"I miss you, and I still love you."

"Nothing has changed."

She explained the whole story to him, the reason why she wasn't with Alden. He told her that there weren't many sisters who could give up the man they loved like that.

"Patsy never knew, and I want to keep it that way."

He pulled her to him, the spark they had when they met was still there. He told her he didn't want lose her from of his life.

"That wouldn't be fair on you – knowing what you know…"

"Zella, please. I love you, I don't care how you feel about Alden."

"No, Michael, it would never work. You *would* care and it would come between us. I don't want to hurt you."

"You can't live loving someone you can't have. You have to let yourself live and get over Alden… be happy with someone else, ME… Zella, let that someone be *me.*"

He kissed her cheek, not wanting to let her go. He pulled her closer and pleaded with her to give them another chance. She tells him she couldn't, it would end in disaster, that's the last thing she wanted to happen.

She knew she had to be strong and send him away. He looked so unhappy when he left. He turned back to her to tell her she knows where he is if she ever changed her mind.

After Michael got back to London, he left his job with Ingrid and joined *Summer Sleek* Photography Agency. Jake Summers had asked him to join his team a year ago but he had never taken him up on the offer but now, looking for change, he asked Jake if it was still open and then jumped at the chance.

His first photoshoot in his new role was with Elaine Crystal. Michael thought she was beautiful, those long, shapely legs and that long blonde mane gently falling around her face as she moved her head. Her eyes were the deepest blue, it was like looking in to the ocean. He got some fabulous shots of her and she was so naturally funny, no wonder she was at the top of her field.

The following week he got to take photographs of Vivian Towers and Millicent Lee. Vivian was every photographer's dream, her stunning looks and raven black hair that sat around her shoulder cradling her beautiful face, her beautiful big, dreamy violet eyes and stunning figure, she simply captivated her audience, the camera loved her. Unfortunately Millicent had to work hard to get even close to Vivian's perfect poses, it just didn't come as naturally as it did for Vivian.

Michael got lost in what he was doing and took way more pictures of Vivian than he had been asked for, but Jake didn't mind. He particularly liked a looking over the shoulder pose from Vivian. He knew Matt would love that picture of his wife and had it blown up for him.

Chapter 30

Alden had just finished packing his bag ready to leave but he didn't realise Patsy was watching him. He was deep in thought staring at something. She must have made a noise or something to make him jump. He snapped his wallet shut rather too quickly making Patsy very suspicious. What did he not want her to see?

"When are you coming home?"

"When I get back."

"That's no answer."

"Well… It's the only one you're getting."

"What are you hiding?"

"Don't know what you're talking about."

"In your wallet…"

"See ya …."

She knew he was up to something and she was going to find out one way or another. Then a little light went on in her head, she would go to London. When the coast was clear, she headed straight round to Mary's.

"Were going to London."

"London? What for?"

"I want to know what Alden is up to."

"Working…?"

"I think he's with *her*."

"Who…?"

"That woman."

Mary pointed out that she had her own life and wasn't going to drop everything when Patsy snapped her fingers.

"Are you coming or not?"

"No… I think you were wrong to do what you did to Alden."

"Fine. I'll go by myself."

"Just let him go. He doesn't love you, he never did."

"This is because you're seeing Melvin – you don't have any time for me anymore."

"You were the same you when you met Alden. Alden this, Alden that, that's all I ever heard. I'm am so pissed off with all your fucking dramas, it's all about *you* all of the time, I'm sick of it. Sort your fuckin life out, grow up!"

"Hmm…I… I …." Patsy spluttered, lost for words. Mary had never ever spoken to her like this before.

Mary carried on, "You are the most selfish bitch I've ever met. Let Alden be with the woman he loves. I'm done with you, don't bother me again. I've always been there for you even when I knew you were in the wrong. Now… if you don't mind…"

Mary turned and slammed the door shut leaving Patsy dumbfounded. She didn't like the way Mary had stood up to her, telling what she thought for a change. Mary had always stood on the sidelines and never said anything, always on Patsy side. No more, it was obvious that she thought Alden was a nice man and Patsy had messed his life up. Now she was in love herself, she could see the other side. Alden should be with the woman he loves and Patsy was totally wrong for what she had done.

Patsy stormed off in a strop. Packing a bag, she headed to London on the train. When she arrived she looked for the Princess Hotel and eventually found it, hoping she could see Zella who was in London on business. There was no sign of Alden but she finally found Zella.

"Patsy? What are you doing here?"

"Looking for Alden."

"He's working…"

Zella gave Patsy her room key and told her to wait in her room for her. As she entered the lift, Derick got in.

"Patsy… what a pleasant surprise."

"Is he with her?"

"Who…?"

"Alden…"

"Hmmm… I'm not sure where he is"

"He's with her, isn't he?"

"Her…?"

"You know who I mean, Derick."

Before he could say another word she lunged at him and kissed him hard on the mouth.

"Patsy…?.What the hell?"

225

"Don't talk!"

He pushed her away, "Patsy!!!"

She forced him against the side of the lift and kissed him again but this time he was kissing her back. As the lift door opened they rushed to his room. There was a desperate urgency to remove each others' clothes. The way he kissed her, the way he touched her excited her in a way that Alden never had. She could tell how much he wanted her by the way he moved his hands over her body. He was gentle, he took his time to please her. Her eyes glistened with excitement and intense fire, her breathing was ragged as he moved back and forth.

"Ahhhh Ohhhh yesssss Ummm…" She moaned as she got close to orgasm.

His rhythm got faster and she groaned louder, sticking her nails into his back as she climaxed again and again. She had never orgasmed as many times before. He made love to for some time before he climaxed. She giggled as he rolled off her and stroked her skin gently.

"You know how I feel about you, don't you, Patsy?"

"I think I might now."

He kissed her softly and they lay back in each other arms, losing track of time. Patsy suddenly jumped up.

"Zella…"

"Zella…?"

"Yes, I was supposed to meet her in her room," she said, jumping out of bed and rushing to get her clothes back on. She leant over and kissed Derick. "I'll see you later."

"I hope so."

When she got back to the room, Zella was waiting outside the door, not looking best pleased.

"Where have you been?"

"Sorry… I got distracted."

"Really! Just let us in."

Zella quickly got changed and shouted from the bathroom, "Does Alden know you're here?"

"No, don't tell him."

"Why…?"

"I don't want him to know I'm here."

"Patsy! Stop playing games!"

"Please Zell, I want to catch him in the act." *'Fine one to talk,'* she thought considering what she had just been up to.

"There's nothing to catch in the act."

"I think there *is*."

Zella rolled her eyes, "OK – but don't you think he will notice you being in the hotel?"

"I'm not staying here."

"Where are you staying?"

"Another hotel down the road."

The whole three days she was there, Patsy and Derick met each other every day. Alden didn't have a clue she was there or what she was up to. Mind you, he wouldn't have cared anyway. Zella hoped that Alden wouldn't mess with any of the models knowing that Patsy was watching him, little did she know that it was Patsy messing around.

As the weeks rolled by, Patsy and Derick had been sneaking around more and more. She was no longer even asking Alden questions about his mystery woman. She had however been spotted with Derick by Hilda, a real busybody who liked a bit of gossip who also liked to add a little bit to her tittle tattle, she was well known for it. As soon as she realised that Alden was home, she made a point of pulling him to one side.

"Hilda, how are you this lovely morning?"

"Alden… my lovey, I need to talk to you."

"Oh… what's wrong?"

"Well… you know me, I don't like to tell tales but I think you should really know what your wife is up to."

Alden looked at her a little baffled and he wasn't particularly bothered either, "*What Patsy's up to. Whatever do you mean?*"

"I saw Patsy down near the river bank, you know, where *Love Cove* is."

"Oh yeah. What was she doing, Hilda?"

"She was cavorting with a young man, that young man was…"

Alden interrupted her, "*Who*, Hilda?"

"Derick…"

"Derick?"

"Yes, your friend Derick."

"When you say *cavorting*…"

"Kissing, touching, you know the sort of thing. She was as bold as brass, she didn't care who saw her."

"Ohhhhh… "Alden gasped, putting his hand to his face playing along with Hilda. The more he gasped the more she went on about it, telling him she was sorry she had to be the one telling him this.

"Thank you for telling me, Hilda."

"She's not like her sister, now she *is* a lovely girl."

"Yes, I quite agree."

She took his hand and told him she was so sorry and it wouldn't go any further, then left him standing there. He watched her walk away, then laughed as he knew that she would spread it round the whole town within half an hour – that's if it wasn't already circulating. He was taken back, however, that Derick hadn't told him anything, seeing as they were mates.

Nevertheless he soon cheered up as he realised this could be the excuse he had been looking for. He could finally get rid of Patsy once and for all. He did worry about Derick, however, he didn't want him to be in the same position he had found himself in.

Chapter 31

Dorian was putting on a fashion show in London and donating the proceeds to the London hospital for Matt. He contacted Zella to see if he could use some of her designs in the show. Zella was delighted and agreed straight away, she thought it was a marvellous thing that Matt and everyone was doing. He also asked Alden if he would do the photography, Alden agreed with no hesitation. There was a lot to do, a lot of organising: venue, models, dresses, hair makeup, not to mention advertising. As well as her designs, Zella helped with everything.

"You're an angel! You, my dear, are destined to be a famous designer! Look at these garments, splendid!" Dorian enthused.

"I like the sound of that!" Zella smiled happily.

Everything was planned down to the smallest detail. Dorian was so fussy about everything, right down to the eyelashes, colour of makeup and hair. He specified exactly how it all had to look with the clothes the models were going to wear. They had sold out, there were a lot of businessmen and women there, and quite a few famous guests too. Dorian was flitting around like a cat on a hot tin roof.

"Oh my. I hope everything looks good tonight."

"It does, Dorian. It's fantastic... it all looks perfect."

"Zella... I adore you," he said, hugging her. Then, peeking through the curtains, he looked at Zella, flapping his arms around. "Oooo... Zella it's got to be a success."

"Dorian... Trust me, its all fabulous. You've worked so hard."

"Let's get this show on the road, ladies." He said, winking at Zella.

She make her way out to the front so she could watch Dorian at work. Suddenly, out of the corner of her eye, she noticed Alden with his camera in his hand. Instinctively, she felt it would be better to simply stay out of his way. She managed it successfully managed during the show but afterwards was another story. He had seen her watching him all the way through the show. He put his camera away then made his way over to the bar where she was standing and tapped her on the shoulder.

"Are you avoiding me?"

"No..." She was, of course.

"I think you are."

"Why would you think that?"

"We *are* allowed to talk to each other, you know"

"I know that."

"Can I get you a drink, then?"

"Alright, yes, thank you."

They made a little small talk about how the show had gone. Alden thought it had gone amazingly and they must have raised a substantial amount of money for the new hospital wing. Then he asks how she got there.

"Train…"

"I'll take you back if like."

"No… you don't have to do that."

"I want to, besides we *are* going back to the same place."

"No… it's fine…"

"Come on Zella, we can get something to eat then drive back."

"I…."

"Come on… please."

She knew it was a bad idea but she agreed in the end.

"Great … Shall we?"

They went over to Dorian to tell him they were heading back as it was long drive back. Dorian kissed Zella on the cheek telling he would call her.

"I look forward to speak to you soon. Bye Alden, make sure my best girl get home safely."

"I will… see you soon, Dorian."

They made their way to a little restaurant in Camden and sat chatting for a while after dinner. Finally, Alden looked at his watch .

"I think we better make a move, it's getting late."

They left the restaurant and made their way to the car. Alden took the back roads toward Chesterfield. Zella wondered way he was driving this way so she asked him.

"I thought it may be quicker this way"

"Oh…"

By this time, it had begun to rain. Suddenly, Alden swore under his breath and pulled over to the side of the road.

"What's wrong? Why we have stopped?"

"I don't know, I'll have a look."

The rain by this time was really heavy and he was getting soaked as he shuffled to the front of the car. He lifted the bonnet to see what was wrong but couldn't see anything obvious. He went to drop the bonnet but didn't move his hand out of the way quick enough and trapped his fingers.

"OUCH… Shit!"

Zella got out of the car when she heard his yell.

"Alden are you alright?"

"Noooooo… I think I've broken my finger."

What with the rain and the dark it was impossible to see Alden's hand, however she did see what she thought was a barn.

"Let's go over there. I think I see a barn, we can wait in there till the rain stops."

Alden went round to the boot of his car clutching his injured hand, clearly in a lot of pain.

"There should be a torch in there…"

Zella grabbed the torch and they made their way to the barn. They were soaked to the skin, shivering and covered in mud. They found some hay they could sit in to keep warm and Zella looked through her bag looking for something to wrap Alden's fingers in as they were bleeding. She managed to find two small pieces of wood to make a temporary split and bandaged his hand up..

"This is the second time we've been stranded together."
He smiled.

"Yeah …"

"I couldn't wish to be stranded with anyone better than you," he said, touching her face gently. "I love you Zella"

She looked into his eyes. "This is an awful mess."

"You still love me, don't you?"

"I've always loved you, Alden." She sighed.

"So… what do we do?"

"There's nothing we can do."

"Yes… there is."

He leant in to kiss her, emotions takes control. Her resistance fell away as she kissed him back, deeper and deeper as they lay back in the hay. He began to remove her wet clothes, slowly, then pulled off his own. He leant forward to kiss her while stroking her soft skin, gently brushing his fingers over her breasts. His eyes gleamed as his mouth caresses her throat, his proximity was overwhelming. His body pressed down on her, moving between her thighs. His erection was hot and throbbing as he pushed himself inside her. He dropped his hand to her hips and she started moving slowly against him, back and forth. Her orgasm, when it came, shook her entire body. With one hard thrust after another, a shuddering spasm shot through her body, the pleasure becoming more intense as he reached climax as well. He rolls slowly off her smiling with pleasure and they drifted asleep in the hay, enveloped in each other's arms.

The sunlight woke Zella up. She jumped up, realising it was the next morning and shook Alden's arm.

"Alden, Alden. Wake up"

"What… what is it?"

"It's, morning… We've been here all night."

"It's OK…"

"No, we need to get some to look at the car so we can get you to the hospital to get those fingers looked at"

"Its fine. I'll just put the wire back on to the battery…"

"What…?"

She was so angry. She grabbed her clothes, desperately getting dressed as quickly as she could..

"Zella…?"

"You did this on purpose?"

"How else was I supposed to get you alone, make you open up?"

"Take me home!"

"Zella, wait."

"No! Take me home now. You have just made me betray my sister, how could you do that?"

"She's sleeping with Derick."

"She wouldn't do that!"

"Yes… she would! Like she lied about being pregnant, everything that happened to us is because of her."

"You're lying about everything. She wouldn't do that… she lost that baby."

"No… Zella, I'm not."

"Take me home!" She screamed angrily.

Zella sat in silence all the way home, she felt so ashamed, he just couldn't get through to her. He dropped her off without a word between them. He did, however, need to go to the hospital. In fact he'd broken two of his finger, cutting one of them very badly. All he knew was that he had to see Zella again even though she was so angry with him it would be impossible to get her to look at him, never mind talk to him.

Patsy had been with Derick and hadn't even realised that Alden hadn't come home that night

Although Zella didn't want to believe what Alden had said about Patsy, something in the back of her mind was telling her to investigate so, a few days later, she decided to lay in wait for Patsy and follow her.

Patsy led her straight to Derick's. She saw him embrace her sister with a very passionate kiss. She couldn't believe her eyes. What Alden had said was true but Zella needed to be extra sure. She waited for Patsy to leave, which was some considerable time later, then she crossed the road to Derick's and banged on the door. He answered the door adjusting his trousers .

"Zella... What are you doing here?" He looked round nervously.

"It's OK, Patsy has gone."

"Patsy?"

"Yes, Patsy."

Derick sighed heavily, knowing he and Patsy have just been caught out.

"You'd better come in." He said nervously.

After putting the kettle on he asked her how long she had known. Zella explained that Alden had tried to tell her but she thought he was lying. Derick shook his head.

"Alden knows?"

"Yes…"

"I love your sister, Zella."

"She's married."

"Yes… to a man who doesn't love her… because he loves *you*."

"How do you know that?" She asked, taken aback.

Derick told her Alden had told him he had always loved her and, while he was at it, confirmed that virtually everything that Patsy had said and done was a lie. Zella stood there in shock at what Derick was telling her.

"I've told Patsy I love her and I want to marry her. I asked her why she holds on to Alden when he wants someone else"

"What was her answer?"

"I don't think she knows herself, but it's me she wants deep down. Alden is an infatuation. She will realise it sooner or later."

"But…, Ohhhh I'm so confused."

"What are you going to do?"

"I don't know."

She need to think and process it all. She couldn't understand why Patsy would say she was pregnant when she wasn't.

It seemed all Patsy had done was to lie – to Alden, their mother and to her. She had no idea who her sister was anymore, she had not been brought up to be so deceitful.

This changed everything for Zella. She needed to talk to Alden but how to go about it? She had to think what to do. She needed to apologise to him but she was still angry with for tricking her over the car like that, but at least she now understood why he had done it. She had never really given him the chance to explain anything properly. She couldn't believe how stupid and stubborn she had been. She did love him and she always had.

The following morning, she made her way to the factory early to speak to Peggy and tell her she would be back a little later.

"OK… see you in a while then."

"See you later."

"Oh Zell, you have remembered that Carlos is over today?"

"Yeah… I won't be long."

Then made her way to Alden house she spotted Patsy leaving for work and headed over knocking on the looking around Alden had opened the door

"Zella…?"

"We need to talk."

"Come in… Zella, I'm sorry."

"Alden, please let me say what I need to say…"

"Alright…"

She was just about to tell him she was sorry and that she still loved him when Patsy walked back in.

"Zella… what are you doing here?"

"I came to see you and to see how Alden's finger is."

"Ohhhh… How did you know that Alden had trapped his finger in the car door?"

Zella had to think fast. "I saw him on his way to the hospital."

"Ohhhh I see, so what did you come to see me for?"

"Uhhhh, I wanted to know if you wanted to go shopping."

"I can't, I'm going to work… but why don't you come with me and I buy you a pot of tea."

"Yeah that would be lovely."

Patsy reached for her purse and pointed out she wouldn't be going anywhere without it, then giggled, taking Zella's hand.

"Bye, Alden."

"Bye…"

After he heard the door shut, he hit the table, "Fuck!"

He thought he could try to see Zella tomorrow but then he remembered he had to go over to Bradford. It seemed like everything was stacked against them in one way or another.

Chapter 32

Kenneth was throwing a special dinner and dance for his team. The paper had hit the number one slot and he wanted to celebrate. Everyone had to bring someone with them. Derick, not being able to take Patsy for obvious reasons, had to find himself a date. Alden really didn't want to take Patsy himself but had to had, for equally obvious reasons. He told her she needed to look good as she would be with a lot of other wives so she decided to consult Zella. Zella really knew her stuff when it came to this sort of thing.

"Zell, you need to help me look *spectacular*."

"Special occasion?" She asked curiously

"I'm going to a dinner dance with Alden."

"Ohhhh, Come on, then. I've got something that's just perfect for you."

They went into the bedroom and Patsy sat patiently on the bed while Zella went through the wardrobe, pulling one dress out after another.

"Here we are." She pulled out a pearl sequined, pop over gown.

"Ohhhh... Zella this is beautiful"

Zella smiled. "Come on, let me do your hair and make-up. Will Derick be at this dinner and dance?"

"Hmmm... Yes, I think so."

"I see..."

When Zella had worked her magic, Patsy looked at herself in the mirror.

"Zella you are the best"

"I hope you have a lovely evening."

Zella was dying to ask Patsy why she had lied but she decided not to not just yet, although what she was waiting for she really didn't know.

Thank you Zell... I do love you, you know."

Patsy headed back home and finished getting ready. She looked stunning but, of course, it went unnoticed by Alden. Derick's eyes nearly fell out of his head when he saw her and he whispered how beautiful she looked .

"Where's your date?" Alden asked.

"Couldn't get one in time."

Alden smirked, "Really... " He shook his head. "I'm going to mingle."

"What about me?" "Patsy asked.

"Derick will take care of you, I'm sure" He smirked again.

"Come on, Patsy. Let's go dance on the old dance floor."

As they danced cheek to cheek, Derick told her he thought it was time for her to tell Alden she wanted a divorce.

"I will... But not tonight."

"Tomorrow... Patsy."

He meant it he wanted everything out in the open so they could all move on. He wasn't going to be messed around or play second fiddle to anyone any more. Patsy nodded. On the other side of the room Alden was busy chatting to some of the team. Kenneth commented on how attractive Patsy was.

"Yeah…"

"You must trust Derick an awful lot leaving him with your wife like that."

"To be really honest Ken, Patsy and I are not really working."

"Ohhhh, I'm sorry."

"No, don't be."

At that moment Derick joined them at the bar. Derick was ordering drinks for Patsy and himself, then put his hand on Alden's shoulder.

"I need to tell you something, Alden."

"Not now"

Back at the table Patsy felt like a cigarette. Reaching down into Alden's pockets looking for his packet she found instead his wallet. Remembering how secretive he had been over it, she pulled it out and, opening it, she found a piece of paper folded up. She slowly opened it and read it.

'To my darling, I can't do this anymore, I can't live this lie, and I love you so much, I know you feel it too.'

Love you always Alden xxx'

She was horrified she stood up, steam coming from every orifice and looked round the room. She spotted Alden, he was chatting to the girls from the office, his boss and the rest of the team. Derick gasped as he spotted Patsy coming over and the look she had on her face. She marched straight past Derick and gave Alden such a slap across the face. The handprint must have burned his face, it looked as if his face was on fire.

"You Bastard!" She shouted, waving the note at him.

"What are you doing?" snatching the note from her hand.

"Who is this to, I smell her on you every time you come home."

"What are you on about? You are embarrassing me." He said, grabbing her arm

"Who is she? I demand to know" She pulled her arm violently away.

"Who is she? You really want to know?" Alden was about to open Pandora's box.

"Yes…"

"Oh I don't think you do, but here it comes…"

"Tell me!" She interrupted angrily.

Derick pulled Patsy away, "Not here Patsy." Everyone was staring, they really didn't know where to put themselves.

"Alright…. I'll give you a clue; I was in Paris, Milan and London with her."

"No you weren't, Zella would have told me."

Alden laughed

"Don't you dare laugh at me, who is she?"

"Maybe this will give it away, she was in Austria."

"No she wasn't… we would have…"

Patsy stopped suddenly in mid-sentence realising, he was talking about her sister. She looked horrified.

"You're talking about Zella… No, No, No! Stop it… Zella wouldn't do that, *she's my sister*."

"That's who I'm in love with, that's who the note is to… Zella is the one I've always been in love with all this fucking time."

"Stop it, stop it, just stop – You're a liar."

"No… I'm not."

Derick tried to pull Patsy away but she got herself loose from his grip and slapped Alden hard across the face again.

"I hate you, I hate you. I want a divorce! Take me home, Derick."

Alden laughed, "Which one of us is going to file for divorce for adultery? I know all about lover boy here."

Derick turned and looked at Alden. "Alden I'm so…"

"You knew I knew … And you are welcome to her. I'm now going to get my Zella" Alden grabbed his coat and stormed out, leaving everyone with their mouths open at the commotion.

Arriving back home Patsy sat down in shock. Derick put the kettle on to make some tea.

"Zella… How could she? *She's my sister*." She began to sob uncontrollably. Derick sat down next to her and hugged her. "How could she, why would she? I love my sister but she has betrayed me."

The tears rolled down Patsy face in an endless flow, her eyes filled with emotion. The hurt she felt turned in to anger, there was no forgiveness. Her eyes had narrowed until they were cold.

"I hate her, I hate them both!"

"Patsy… The truth is that you caused all this."

"I caused all this …?"

"Yes, you did."

"Are you taking sides with them?"

"No, but all this, well it's a total mess."

He made her a strong cup of tea with lots of sugar seeing as she had just had the shock of her life.

"Come on, drink your tea, and go to bed. Things may seem a little clearer tomorrow."

"I need a stiff drink, not fuckin' tea… And things are pretty clear *now.*"

"No… they're not, Patsy."

"You knew didn't you?"

"Yeah…"

"Omg Ohhhhh….. Leave! Get the fuck out!"

"Come on, Patsy, you're not little miss innocent yourself. You've been fooling around with me for months."

She began to cry again. "I thought you were on my side, I thought you loved me."

"I do… but you need to face some facts, like you're not initially blameless in all this. You need to grow up. I do love you and I want to marry you."

She put her head down and agreed "I know, I know, but Zella I'll never forgive"

All the while, across the other side of town, Alden reached Zella's and he banged frantically on the door.

"Zella…" He shouts desperately, "Zella come on, come to the door."

245

Finally, the light in the hall came on and he heard her taking the chain from the door.

"Zella, it's me!" He shouted through the letterbox. As the door opened he tried to explain. "I'm sorry Zella... but Patsy knows about us."

She looked at him, taking his face in her hands. She kissed him full on the mouth and taking his hand she led him into the house.

"You're not angry with me?"

"No... I know what you told me is all true. I'm sorry I didn't believe you, I never give you a chance to explain all those years ago."

"It doesn't matter anymore, we can start again," With that, he took her in his arms and kissed her. "I love you."

"Alden, I love you, I always have."

Their kisses deepened. There was an urgency to get to the bedroom, she led him in, stumbling and staggering to the bed.

The urge to become naked was uncontrollable His warm lips descended on hers, his kiss even deeper than before. His fingers skated down her skin sudden urge of passion ran through their bodies his hips moved between her thighs as he thrust himself in to her, moving slowly back and forth, she sighed with pleasure. Their passion was hot like an inferno. The more she moaned he thrust deeper and faster his hands firm on her hips to hold his rhythm. She wanted him so much she didn't want it to end. As they orgasmed they both flopped back on the bed.

Alden looked across at her triumphantly, breathlessly telling her he was hungry. She rolled her eyes and giggled, throwing her dressing gown on.

"You're hungry?"

"Yes… I've worked up an appetite." He said, jumping out of bed and putting his clothes on telling her he would go get some fish and chips.

"Fish and chips…? At this hour…?"

"Yeah…it's not late, the chippy will still be open."

Zella told him she would put the kettle on and he kissed her gently on her forehead.

"I'll be back in a minute."

He'd been gone no more than five minutes. She was about to butter some bread when she heard an awful screech and one almighty bang. She ran to the door looking out to see what had happened. She grabbed a passing women to ask what had happened, she told her a truck had crashed, someone was hurt. She grabbed her coat and keys, still in her dressing gown and slippers, and went looking for Alden. She saw the over turned truck and looked round desperately. Suddenly she saw someone on the road, lifeless.

Her heart sank when she came to the horrifying realisation it was Alden, "OH NO!" She screamed, "No, no, no, ALDEN!"

A police officer pushes her back, "Nothing to see, miss."

"That's my……"

"Is he your husband?" He interrupted.

"Yes…"

The officer lets her through to be with him

"Alden, please be alright. I can't lose you. Please, please, Alden, PLEASE!" Tears streamed down her face like a wild brook.

The ambulance arrived to rush him to the hospital and straight into theatre. Zella waited and waited. It was hours before they finally took him to the intensive care ward.

"Mrs Pearce?"

"Hmm… No."

"Well, I can't really tell you much, it really has to be his family."

"I'm his sister in law."

"Is your sister here?"

"No… but I will go get her if you need her to be here."

"Yes, she needs to be here."

She caught a taxi to Patsy's to tell her about Alden but all she got from Patsy was a slap across the face yelling at her that she didn't want to talk to her nor would she go to see Alden, before slamming the door in her face.

"You will talk to me!" She shouted through the letter box, "Patsy open this door!"

"I have nothing to say to you."

Patsy open the door only to push Zella away.

"You are coming with me to the hospital."

"No, I'm not!"

"Oh yes you are. Even if I have to drag you there by your hair, you are going."

Patsy shook her head and was about to close the door when Zella put her foot in the way.

"Don't fuckin' push me Patsy, because you know I will drag you there."

Patsy knew she meant every word. Derick came to the door.

248

"What's going on?" and noticing Zella, "Zella?"

"She has to come to the hospital."

"Why... What's wrong?"

Zella explained to Derick what had happen. Patsy kept saying she didn't care and he deserved everything he had got. Zella's face went blood red and steam was positively come from her ears.

"I swear if you don't shut you fucking mouth, I with shut it for you!"

"Patsy that's an awful thing to say. Alden is my best friend, my brother, he's the only family I have, we need to go." added Derick.

"Thank you Derick"

"How bad is it?" Derick asked, clearly worried.

"He's in a bad way."

"Get your coat, Patsy, we'll go in the car."

All the way to the hospital Patsy glared at Zella. After they had been to the hospital, Patsy was going to tell Zella exactly what she thought of her. Zella, knew what was coming but she didn't care about Patsy. Her thoughts were only for Alden.

Arriving at the hospital they waited for the doctors to see them. They immediately took Patsy into a side room to speak to her. He told her that Alden had a spinal and head injury but at this stage they didn't know if he would pull through, and even if he did he may never walk again depending on the damage, only time would tell. Patsy was shocked to say the least. When she appeared from the room, Zella jumped up.

"What did the doctor say?"

Patsy turned to Derick and told him what the doctor had said. She totally dismissed Zella she didn't even look at her, as they walked out of the hospital.

"We'll go home and get some rest then come back in the morning"

"How the hell do I get my divorce?"

"That's all you are concerned about?" Zella growled at her.

"Was I talking to you?"

"He nearly died, he still might… Then you won't need to worry, will you?"

"I don't care."

"Patsy…." Derick shouted angrily. "What did we talk about earlier? Alden is my family, don't say things you will regret Patsy, I'm really not liking the Patsy I'm seeing right now."

Zella was so angry she shouted out, "You are a piece of work, do you know that? You're a liar, a cheat and the most selfish person I have ever known… and *you are not my sister.*"

"You stole my husband."

"I… what…? He was never yours to steal."

"He was my husband, Zella."

"Only because you faked your pregnancy, you deceitful little bitch!"

"I lost that baby."

"Omg… you are *still* lying. You were never pregnant, you are just a scheming little bitch. I know the truth, I gave up the man I loved for you."

"You are a slut."

Zella moved toward pushing her face up to Patsy's, "*I'm the slut…?*"

Derick tried desperately to defuse the situation by standing between them.

"Now, Now ladies… Come on, this is not going to help Alden."

"She won't… all she's bothered about is her fuckin' divorce."

"Fuck you, Zella"

Zella pushes Derick out of her way and grabbed Patsy.

"Right enough…" and he put himself in between them again, pushing them apart. He could see this situation turning in to a slapping match.

"First, this is not helping and second, the foul language that is coming out of your mouths is disgraceful. You are supposed to be ladies." He shouted angrily. With his hand firmly on their arms holding them apart, "You should both be ashamed of yourselves.

They both looked down at their feet apologetically and Zella told Derick he was right and he should he take Patsy home, she really couldn't bear looking at her. Patsy agreed on one thing with Zella, she wanted to go home. Derick asked Zella how she was she getting home. She told him she was fine, she would be staying at the hospital. He told her he would see her the next day after he had seen their boss.

"Don't bring *her* with you."

"Don't worry, I won't be back."

"Good… I don't want you anywhere near me."

"Slut…"

"I swear…. I'm going to knock your head off your shoulders in a minute."

"Slut, Slut, Sluuuut…!"

Zella was just about to hit Patsy when Derick bundled her into the car. Zella watched them disappear before she went back in to sit with Alden. She was there all night even though the nurse told her to go get some rest and to eat something. She called Carlos to let him know where she was and he told her he to keep him informed about Alden.

Chapter 33

Weeks passed and Alden lay so still, there was no apparent response to anything although she could see his chest move up and down. It was just a relief to know he was breathing. Derick went in every other day and Florence and Harold came from Devon to see Alden and to see if she could sort this very big problem between her two girls. She had been to see Patsy and, of course, she give the performance of a lifetime, telling her mother about how Zella had stolen her husband. Florence knew it wasn't quite the way Patsy told the story. She had always thought that Alden was the young man that Zella was going to bring home to meet her and somehow it all suddenly changed. When Florence and Harold arrived at the hospital Zella had her head on the bed holding Alden's hand

"Zella… darling."

"Mum…" and she burst into tears.

"Zella, sweetheart," placing her arms around, Zella hugging her tight.

"I'm so sorry… we have both let you down"

"Zella... I knew that Alden is the one you loved."

Zella was totally shocked by what her mother had just said and asked how.

"You both think I don't notice things... but I know Alden is in love with you and he was the one you were going introduce to me, but how Patsy ended up marrying him is where I got lost."

"I didn't want Patsy to get hurt."

"You see, you are such a considerate girl. I love you both so dearly but Patsy rushes headlong into things. You are the sensible one, always thinking thing through."

"It's such a mess."

"It will sort itself out, I'm sure. I warned Alden not come between you girls."

Florence and Harold Stayed over as long as they could. Sadly, she hadn't been able to make her girls see sense. She did, however, find out about Patsy and Derick, courtesy of Mrs busybody Hilda, who seemed to take great pleasure in telling Florence all about Patsy and Derick. Florence simply told her she didn't think it was any business of hers and should not be discussing it with everyone. Hilda repeated that she thought it was a disgrace and Patsy should be ashamed of herself. Harold told her nobody had asked for her opinion and should kindly keep it to herself.

The weeks turned into months and they moved Alden to a side ward where Zella would sit with him for hours, pleading with him to wake up. There were no signs of him regaining consciousness. By this time the Russell family were the talk of the town, people stopped and stared at Patsy when she walked down the street.

That's her… she's the one that is carrying on with her husband's mate while he's in a hospital bed fighting for his life"

"Ohhhh… yes I've heard they are all at it."

"What do ya mean?"

"Well…. I've heard that the other sister at it to. She s been having an affair with the husband."

"Well I never, what is this world coming to? I blame this new age hippie culture and free love stuff that seems to be coming in."

"Shocking…"

Even when Patsy was at work, she would see them outside, sitting sniggering and whispering, like a bunch of old cackling witches.

One afternoon Hilda was telling a lady what a disgrace it was, when Peggy overheard her telling some story or another about Zella.

"Excuse me, should you be gossiping like that?"

"Sorry?"

"Well… do you have all the facts or are you just making them up as you go along?"

"I beg your pardon?"

"Facts…. Do you have them?"

"No… But…"

"Well, *shut up then!*" Peggy shouted her down.

Hilda and the lady she was talking to looked down their noses at Peggy and tut tutted.

"Yeah… You can look down your nose at me all you want. You're both vultures. You haven't got a clue what or why or what that family are going through, so keep your fat traps shut ladies!"

"Ohhhhh.... How rude."

Patsy smiled at Peggy and thanked her for sticking up for them.

Meanwhile Alden finally opened his eyes. Looking round the room, he was a little confused and felt like he'd been hit by a ten ton truck, not far from the truth, in fact. He wondered where he was and he looked across to side of the bed, only to see Zella. She hadn't notice he had woken. She had his hand in hers stroking it tenderly, pleading for him to recover.

"Where am I?" He said, croakily.

Zella started and looked up at him. She was so relieved he had woken up.

"Ohhhh...Alden..."

"What am I doing here?"

"You had a very bad accident, darling."

"I...I...can't...feel my legs. *Why can't I feel my legs?*" He sounded so scared, his voice trembled as he spoke and a look of despair spread across his face.

"I'll go get the doctor," she said, interrupting him, trying to reassure him.

Zella came back with a nurse and, as they entered the room, Alden had a full blown seizure. The nurse shouted frantically for the doctor who was, luckily not far away. They asked Zella to wait outside the room for a moment.

She waited nervously outside the room whilst they attended to him. It was only a few minutes but felt like hours. She was shaking with fear and panic, pacing up and down until the doctor and nurse finally came out.

"You can go back in now"

She went back in to find Alden deathly white, his eyes frozen dark and motionless, it worried her enormously but he was at least stable. As the days went on, he cut himself off putting himself in a darker, deeper place. He felt so hopeless, the inward tears and the uncertainty made him retreat into himself. Zella asked Derick to visit him as often as he could to try and bring him out of himself again.

"Hi, Alden."

Alden looked at Derick. It was obvious that he didn't remember Derick or who he was. He tried again.

"Magnet…?"

"*Magnet?* I don't understand."

"Magnet is your nickname."

"Why? Who are you then?"

"Derick… *Snippet*."

"So are we friends?"

"Yeah… we are best buds, we grew up together and you my friend, you are a journalist."

"Are you a Journalist too?"

"Yeah… I'm a Photo Journalist, a cameraman."

Alden had many questions and Derick filled him in on all he wanted to know. The one thing Alden didn't ask about was if he was married, had any children, or was in a relationship. When Derick left, Zella was just on her way in and Derick told her he had no memory of any of his life, and he wasn't sure whether he should have mentioned Patsy or not. She told him she would talk to the doctor. She asked the nurse about what the doctor had said to Alden, and she replied that the doctor had warned him he may not walk again, but they couldn't know for sure until the swelling around the base of his spine went down. She was very positive and reassured Zella that this could happen at any time. It might be a very long term or could equally be just a short term memory block, only time would tell.

When she went in to the room, Alden just lay there looking out of the window like a statue. He felt lost and empty inside, he simply didn't know who he was.

"Alden …?"

He turn his head towards her and gazed at her. He was very confused and asked if he knew her

"I'm Zella."

He shook his head and shrugged his shoulders, "I… I…"

"Alden, it's me."

"No… I…I…"

Zella's heart sank, she was devastated. Her eyes began to fill, the tears running down her face. Eventually, she told him she'd leave and let him get some rest, hoping tomorrow would be a better day. He didn't see how tomorrow could be any better than today. The next day was just the same and so on day after day, week after week.

Zella was there rain or shine. He would get very angry for no reason and one day he got so angry he had another seizure. The nurses rushed in after Zella franticly shouted. She seemed to wait in the waiting room forever. When the nurse came out, she asked if she could go back in.

"Yes, of course."

She stood up and then she went really dizzy. The nurse told her to sit back down and she would get her a glass of water. She came back and as Zella drank the water she asked how she was feeling.

"Yeah, OK, I must have needed a drink."

"Or you are exhausted. You are here day in day out, you need some rest."

"I'll rest when I know Alden is alright."

"That's all very nice but you will make yourself ill."

"I'll be fine…"

With everything that had happen over the past four mouths Zella had noticed that she had missed her periods for the past four months. Going dizzy like that meant there was a big possibility that she could be pregnant. Getting to her feet, she went back into Alden. He looked at her long and hard.

"Why are you here?"

"Why… but I love you."

"Please go…"

"Alden…. *Please*."

"Get out, I don't want you here, *I don't know you!*"

Heartbroken, Zella ran out crying. After everything that they had gone through to be together, she felt everything was *her* fault.

Day after day she went to him , day after day he told her to go away and leave him alone. Finally, she decided to leave it for a day. Instead of the hospital, she went to her doctor, thinking she'd better find out if she was pregnant. A test proved it, the doctor confirmed that she was four months pregnant. She thought it was time to tell Alden everything that had happened between then, after all he needed to know he was about to become a father. Whether he would take it all in would be another matter.

The next morning she made her way to the hospital again to be sent away. How on earth was she going to tell him anything if he wouldn't let her stay to talk to him? On her way home she stopped to see the headline of the papers.

Weekly whisper

Vivian and Matt Adams *have announced the birth of their son. Vivian gave birth to* Luke *this morning at 3am, weighing in at 7lbs 8oz. The couple are said to be over the moon. Matt left the hospital beaming from ear to ear and told the press that mother and son were both doing great, and he couldn't wait to get them both home.*

She smiled. She was so happy for Vivian and Matt, at least someone was happy.

Meanwhile Alden did get to talk to a visitor that day. Patsy had gone to see him about their divorce.

"Hello… Alden"

Alden stared at her blankly.

"Fuck me, how many women are there? Which one are you?"

"I'm your wife."

"My… What…?"

"Your wife… Patsy."

"Are we happily married?"

"No… we should never have got married."

"So why did we?"

"Long story, but I want a divorce, so do you?"

260

He looked at her again concentrating on her face. He suddenly had a huge sense that he knew who she was and what had been happening.

"Yes, yes… you should get the paperwork in order then I'll sign. Then we can be free of each other.

"Alden… Do you know who I am now?"

"No… not really but…"

Things were still a little hazy but he knew he didn't want to be with this woman. Thoughts and images of Zella flooded his mind and he started remembering small things, then important things. One thing he was getting more sure about was Zella and how much he loved her.

Chapter 34

One morning, before Zella left for the hospital, she got a call from Dorian, he wanted to see her. She told him she couldn't get over to London right then and explained about Alden, so Dorian said he would come to Chesterfield, he had something very important to discuss with her.

At the same time, Michael had decided to go to the hospital. The nurse told Alden he had a visitor and Michael popped his head round the curtain.

"Michael?"

"Hello Alden… Wow, you remembered me? "

"Yes as soon as you walked in. To what do I owe the pleasure?"

"I came to see how you were doing. You gave us all a scare."

"I've been better, I can tell you." He laughed

"What have the doctors said?"

"Well… they are not sure if I will walk again."

"I'm sorry, Alden, I really am. Let's hope that isn't the case."

"What are you really here for?"

"I came to see you."

"Michael?"

"You know that Dorian has offered Zella a partnership, don't you?"

"No, I didn't."

Michael went on to tell him what a great opportunity it was and one Zella should take. Alden agreed with him and asked if she had accepted. Michael told him he didn't know.

"She has to."

"I don't think she will, though."

"Why ever not?"

"She won't leave you. She loves you, Alden."

"And you still love her, Michael, don't you?"

"Yes…but I'm not here for that. I just wanted you to know about the partnership deal."

Alden told Michael that Zella would definitely take the deal with Dorian and Michael looked at him curiously, wondering what he was going to do.

"I'll leave you to rest now, Alden. It was good seeing you, take care of yourself and I hope everything turns out right for you."

"Thank,s Michael. Oh, Michael, don't tell Zella about your visit."

"OK, if that's want you want."

"Yep…"

A few moments later, Alden asked his nurse if she could pass him his jacket. He rummaged through the pockets and took his wallet out. Taking a photo out of it, he handed it to the nurse.

"Ooooh… that's you and Miss Russell. You look very much in love."

"She going to be a famous designer one day soon."

"Are you alright, Alden?"

"I can't stand in her way."

He rummaged through his other pockets until he found the letter he had written to her when they were in Paris. He knew what he had to do, and Zella had to take that partnership deal, she just had to.

After her meeting with Dorian, Zella went to the hospital as usual. Alden was sat up in bed.

"Hi…Alden."

He took a deep breath, "What are you here for?"

"To see you, now before you start…"

"Look… Lady… I know you seem to know me, but I don't know who you are."

"Alden…"

"Leave… I don't need your pity. Look Miss… whoever…"

"Zella…"

"Look Miss Zella, I don't want you here. Please leave before I have you removed."

She put her hands to her face as if he'd struck her and tears rolled down her cheeks.

"Why are you being like this, Alden?"

"*Just leave*! …and don't come back – they won't let you in!"

Zella ran out of the room crying and rushed out of the ward. The nurse shouted after her but she didn't turn round, she just ran. She was heartbroken, she couldn't believe he had said those hurtful things to her.

The nurse asked Alden if everything was alright as she had seen Zella leave in such a hurry. She could see that Alden was also upset and he told her he had just told Zella never to come back.

"But, why would you do that?"

"I had to – please can we leave it at that"

"Of course."

"Please don't let her back in. Oh, and the convalescent home with the rehabilitation that you mentioned, count me in."

He asked to get move as soon as possible, he didn't want to be at the hospital when Zella came back. The only person who would know where he was would be Derick.

Zella thought if she left him for a few days he might change his mind. Derick went round to Zella's to see how Alden was and, tearfully,she explained what had happened. He was shocked, he knew how much Alden loved Zella. She went on to tell him about the partnership with Dorian and how she didn't feel she could take it.

"But why not?"

"Alden needs me… and not only that, I have just had it confirmed I'm pregnant."

"Have you told Alden you're having his baby?"

"He doesn't remember me so how what good would it do?"

Derick told her not to worry, he was sure that Alden would get his memory back soon. The next day he went to the hospital.

"Hi Al…"

"Derick, my mate."

"You know who I am?"

"Yeah, why"

"So how do you not remember Zella?"

Alden sighed heavily, "You've seen Zella? Is she alright?"

"What the fuck are you playing at, Alden? You have only just got her back in your life, why this?" He asked, not understanding.

"I can't walk, I don't know if I ever will again and Dorian has offered her a partnership. I can't stand in her way."

"She's turned it down."

"No! No… no. *Why?*"

"She loves you and wants to care for you… you need to talk to her."

"No! Don't say anything to her, she must take the partnership now, I was so hurtful, she must take it!"

Derick shook his head. He didn't understand what Alden was doing. He loved Zella, he always had. He couldn't believe that he'd turned her away.

Within a few days Alden had been transferred to another hospital. When Zella found out, she was so upset she couldn't believe it was all happening. It was as if the Gods were trying to keep them apart. She did, however, have to face facts, she was going to be a single mum and she simply had to get on with it.

❧ ❧

Zella had to tell Florence she was about to become a mother, making her a grandmother. Surprisingly, she took it all in her stride. Zella really thought her mother would have been disappointed in her.

"I'm happy for you, darling. You *are* happy?"

"Yes, mum, I'm happy."

"How's thing with you and Patsy? Please tell me you have made up."

"I'm sorry, mum but no."

"I was hoping you two would be alright now."

"How is Harold?"

"He's doing just fine and you, my love, are changing the subject."

"I know. I'm sorry, mum, but Patsy won't talk to me and frankly I don't want to talk to her either."

"Does Alden know about the baby?"

"No… I don't know where he is. I've just found out he has been transferred to another hospital… but I don't know where."

"Ohhhh…darling, I'm so sorry."

"Nothing I can do, it looks like it's just going to me and my baby."

Chapter 35

The swelling on Alden's spine had finally started to go down and he began to regain feeling in his legs. He was relieved, to say the least, and the hospital had told him there was nothing more they could for him, he was well enough to be taken to new convalescent home where he would get the physiotherapy he needed.

"Hampshire. It's a new place, an amazing facility/"

Alden smiled.

"It will be very good for you, Alden."

"Will I walk again?"

"You have feeling in your legs, that's a good sign."

Alden was feeling hopeful and nervous all at the same time as the ambulance turned in to the grounds of Cherry Tree Lodge. The whole place was surrounded by big oak trees and an avenue of blossom trees leading to a lake. The sweet aroma of the pink blossom filled the air. It was tranquil and peaceful. He'd already spotted the shops and the country pubs on the way in to the village and made it his goal to walk to the nearest pub and have a pint of beer with Derick.

He had set his divorce from Patsy in motion by signing the paperwork that she had given him before he left. The only person who knew where he was was Derick, who had promised to come and see him every week. Alden didn't want anyone to know, especially Zella, and he made Derick swear not to tell her.

"You don't have to come here every week, Derick. I know you must have other things you could be doing."

"You're my friend…"

"Why don't you come every month or so?"

"Why are you pushing me away?"

"I don't want pity or to be a burden anyone, for that matter."

"You're not… It will get lonely with no visitors."

Alden told him about a fellow patient he had met, Sid Tanner. They would sit in the garden and Sid would tell him about World War One.

"Always after a story…?"

"You know me." He laughed.

"Are you sure you don't want me to come every week? I feel as if I'm abandoning my pal."

"Don't be daft… This way you can tell me how I'm progressing."

"OK, if you are sure. Just tell me if you change your mind."

Alden smiled and told him to go live his life. As he was leaving, Alden waved him goodbye. Derick couldn't help feeling bad about not seeing him for weeks on end, they had been friends for such a long time. He couldn't help thinking about Zella too. He could remember when She and Alden met and how Alden had kept her identity a secret, even from him. And now he'd pushed her away. He knew that if Alden knew about his baby that would change his mind.

❧ ❧

As the months rolled on, Alden was getting stronger and stronger. Derick saw that he was getting back to his old self and he had made it down to the pub with Sid. They would both walk slowly down to the village and have a pint of bitter. They had become good friends and he'd told Sid all about Zella.

"She sound a lovely girl."

"She is, Sid… really lovely."

"Why are you still here then? Why are you not with her?"

"I don't want to ruin her life…"

"Don't let her slip through your fingers like I let my Mathilda go, Alden lad. You'll regret it for the rest of your life. Don't get me wrong, I loved my wife Wilma, but Mathilda… Well, she was my first love."

"What was Mathilda like then?"

"Ohhhhh… beautiful, Alden. She had shoulder length raven hair and violet eyes, and those legs, Oh my, they led straight up to heaven," he chuckled

"She sounds like Vivian Towers"

"Vivian Tower yes… Vivian Towers looks like my Mathilda. Are you having mucky thoughts about my Mathilda, lad?"

"No, she's your girl." Alden chuckled.

270

"That good I thought I was going have challenge you to a duel then, you know the old fisticuff stuffs."

Alden laughed. He really liked Sid, he was so funny and excellent company. The next day was visiting day and he was looking forward to seeing Derick again.

"Hi, it's good to see you, Derick."

"Good to see you."

"Meet my pal, Sid" Alden said as introduced Sid.

"Hello, Derick," Sid said, holding his hand out

Derick shook his hand and told him it was nice to meet him, he'd heard a lot about him.

"Handsome chap, isn't he?" Sid said as he got up from his chair, leaving Alden and Derick to talk.

"You don't have to go," Derick objected.

"I'm going to go and chat up Nurse Price. She's a real looker. You lads don't stand a chance while I'm here." He chuckled to himself, walking away.

"He's a character… a real charmer. He has the nurses eating out of his hand." Alden laughed, totally amused by Sid.

Derick smiled. He knew Alden really liked Sid and he was right, he was quite the character.

"Now, how is my friend?"

"I'm good, Derick."

"You do know that you are a free man now?"

"My divorce has come through?"

"Yeah… and I'm getting married"

Alden congratulated his friend. "Patsy, I presume."

271

Derick smiled then nodded, "Are you not going to ask about Zella?"

Alden shook his head. He just wanted her to be happy, he didn't want to know with whom or with what.

Sid stood at the door shaking his head. Alden was going let Zella slip through his fingers just like he had with Mathilda all those years ago. He couldn't believe history was about to repeat itself.

Meanwhile in Chesterfield

Carlos had made his way to Chesterfield to give Zella the good news about the Paris factory.

"Remember the factory I bought in Paris? Well, we are up and running."

"That's fantastic news, Carlos."

"Which bring me to the proposition I have for you."

"Oooo... sound interesting"

"It is... I want you to run it."

Zella got very excited at the prospect of running the Paris outlet but this soon turned to disappointment as she couldn't see how she could accept the offer.

"Zella, you turned down Dorian's offer... don't let all your dreams die completely."

"But ... How can I do such a demanding job when I'm about to become a mother, a mother on her own I might add. Not to mention where would I live?"

"Do you remember me telling you the factory had an old warehouse attached it?"

"Yes..."

"Well I had that turned into a flat, actually with you in mind."

Zella's eyes brightened back up again Carlos could see the excitement in them.

"What do you think, Zella?"

"Hmmm…Ohhhh… Yes, but what about looking after the baby?"

"You can work from home, get a nanny… Come on, Zella please accept."

"Yesssss!" She shouted clapping her hands with joy, "When do I go?"

"When you are ready."

She spoke to her mum and told her news. Florence was delighted for her but she wanted her to have the baby first, she didn't want Zella traveling while she was so heavily pregnant. What if she needed her mother, what would she do then?

Zella assured her that she wouldn't be going until after the baby was born and that she and Harold could come over to see her and the baby whenever they wanted. Next, she spoke to Derick and gave him her new address in the hope that Alden would regain his memory.

Derick wished her luck and suggested she and Patsy try to sort things out but Zella thought it was too soon. Their feelings for each other were still running high and she thought it might make things worse between them. Perhaps some time in the future.

Zella went into labour a month later and she gave birth to Beverly Rose Russell. She chose Rose as Beverly's middle name because it was her mother's middle name. Beverly weighed in at 6lbs 12oz and she was beautiful with jet black hair. Zella wished that Alden could see his daughter, he would have fallen in love with her instantly. When she brought Beverly home again, the Russell family were the talk of the town.

In fact, the town gossips were talking about Zella and how she was on her own with a baby when Patsy had arrived at work that day.

"What are you talking about my sister for?"

"Ohhhh Ummm… weren't."

"Yes you were, I heard you."

"You heard wrong."

"You are like a bunch of cackling old witches. Have you nothing better to do with yourselves?"

"And you and your sister are little hussies."

"At least we have lived and had some fun, unlike you old bats."

The ladies tut tutted and looked down their snooty noses and waddled out of the shop.

Glowering around, Patsy spotted Dolly in the corner trying so hard not to be noticed. Too late, Patsy has seen her and made her way over to her to point out that she called herself Zella's friend.

"I know that."

"So why were you just sitting there saying nothing? You should have stood up for my sister!"

Dolly put her head down and mumbled that they had a point. Patsy blasted her out and told her she wasn't Zella's friend, she was no better than they were pointing at the

women through the window. Patsy gave Dolly the coldest
of looks and turned away.

Chapter 36

January 1963

Zella was packed and ready to go, finally about start a new
life in Paris with Beverly. Derick offered to take them to the
airport but she refused as she had already booked a taxi.
Derick had told Patsy that this may be her only chance to
see her sister before she let her walk out of her life. Patsy
thought long and hard. She loved Zella and couldn't really
imagine her life without her in it.

"Derick, will you take me to the airport?"

"Yes…" Derick smiled. "I think you have made a wise
  decision"

He was really pleased that Patsy had changed her mind.
They arrived just in time as Zella was just about to go
through to the departure lounge.

"Zella…" Patsy shouted.

Zella turned and saw Patsy waving at her. She walked back
over to her, holding Beverly tight in her arms.

"I… *I love you*, Zella"

Zella threw her arms around Patsy. "I love you too,
  Patsy."

"I couldn't let you go without telling you I'm so sorry I
  caused you all the pain and heartache. It was entirely my
  fault."

"Let's forget it."

"Can I hold my niece?"

Zella passed Beverly over and Patsy gazed down at her.

"She's so beautiful."

"You and Derick must come over and see us."

"We will, and you must come back over for our wedding... I hope Alden soon remembers and finds you, we have all wasted so much time."

Zella kissed her sister tenderly, "I hope you are truly happy, Patsy."

"I am now" she said, smiling at Derick. "... and I hope you will be soon!"

She handed Beverly back after kissing her gently. Waving a tearful goodbye to her and Beverly, Patsy watched Zella until she was out of sight. Turning to Derick, she thanked him for making her see sense and told him he was the best thing that had ever happened to her.

∽   ∾

After boarding, Zella settled Beverly down ready for the short flight. She watched her as she slept, she was so beautiful and she could see Alden in her.

Looking out of the window at the clouds it was like looking at white fluffy cotton wool floating by. After the plane had made its descent, they disembarked and made their way to passport control, then on to the luggage carousel to collect her cases. She found them a taxi, the driver could see Zella was struggling with a baby, cases and the pram so he held the door open and helped in putting everything in the boot. She thanked him and asked him take her to the address Carlos had given her.

After a short drive they came to the factory. The driver looked perplexed.

276

"Je pense que tu as la mauvaise addresse…"

"Sorry, umm… Je m'éxcuse…

"You 'ave the wrong place, certainement"

"No… no – this is it."

"Vous êtes sûr? You sink so?"

"Yes, this is it. *Merci.*"

She paid the driver and he helped her with her cases and pram. Zella climbed the steep staircase that led up to the flat, opening the door looking back at her surroundings, The factory was all closed up, it was getting quite dark and she thought she'd better get Beverly in, fed and to bed. Entering the flat she was pleasantly surprised, It was completely furnished. Miriam had thought of everything, she'd even put up the cot for Beverly.

Zella loved it, she knew that she and Beverly would be happy here. She brought the cases in before feeding Beverly and then put her to bed, it had been a long day.

As she looked round she found the lounge, kitchen and study (so she could work from home), a bathroom and three bedrooms. From the master bedroom you could see a little stone church on one side and a château with a beautiful garden, it was a wonderful view.

Finally able to relax, she made a pot of tea and a cheese sandwich. She had just settled down in the big comfy chair when the phone rang. She wasn't sure who on earth this could be, she didn't know anyone here and she couldn't have given anyone the number because she didn't know it herself.

"Hello…." She said cautiously.

"Zella, you're there then?"

"Carlos!" She said, relieved, and proceeded to tell him she'd got there about an hour before.

"Miriam wants to know if you like what she's had done with the place?"

"I love it. She has quite the eye for interior design."

"Yes she has, we wanted to come over so I can introduce you to all your staff."

"Ohhhh I hope they like me." She giggled nervously.

"They are all so excited to meet you. Miriam said she would watch Beverly for you while you met everyone."

"Ohhhhh thank you, thank you so much."

He told her to get a good night's sleep and they would see her in the morning. She was so pleased that Carlos and Miriam would be there to help her on her first day, however she would need to find a nanny to look after Beverly for a few hours every day so she could spend time in the factory. She thought she had better learn some French too, seeing as she would have to speak with everyone who in the factory, not to mention when she needed to go shopping. So it started, Zella working from home and interviewing suitable nannies.

When Cecilia Badon arrived for her interview Zella liked her immediately and when she said she had been the nanny for the family at the château, Zella was even more impressed. It occurred to her to wonder why Cecilia had left the château and asked her. Cecilia told her she had left because of the myth of the Lady of the Château.

Zella was intrigued and asked her to tell her the story. She began with the beautiful château itself. Built in the 1800s, it had hectares upon hectares of land, including a vineyard. The main house had ten bedrooms and six bathrooms. All the rooms had hand-painted wallpaper, marble fireplaces and harlequin-tiled floors. It had servants' quarters, courtyards, stables and barns together with a beautiful lake. It had been such a beautiful and happy place.

The myth was that the beautiful daughter of the house, Lady Pirrette Beaulieu, had died, suddenly and mysteriously, at the age twenty two. It was said that she had been poisoned. The reason had never been discovered and it was believed that Lady Pirrette roams the corridors every night calling for her lover, Albert Deveau. Zella was captivated by this story but suddenly Beverly woke from her nap.

"Ohhhhh… I have shivers up my spine, that's so sad." and she walked away to get Beverly.

When she came back, Cecilia smiled, "She's so beautiful."

"Thank you."

Cecilia had won Zella over and she was hired on the spot. She was really good with Beverly and Zella was pleased. Cecilia had come highly recommended by the family at the château. They were sorry to lose her but understood her reasons for leaving.

Months passed. The factory was booming and Carlos had made Zella a partner. There had been no word from Derick about Alden but she knew in her heart of hearts he would remember her one day. She had given up her dream of becoming a famous designer because she truly loved him and she was the mother of his daughter. He *had* to remember for Beverly's sake, if nothing else. By now, she had received her invitation to Patsy and Derick's wedding and there she would see her mother and Harold.

She was so happy to see them and, of course, her mother was so happy her daughters had made up and were sister again, instead of enemies. And, of course, she got to see her beautiful granddaughter. She and Harold made such a big fuss when they saw their beautiful Beverly.

"She is such a pretty little thing, so happy"

"Yeah she's always happy Harold, she a delight"

Florence took hold of her, giving her a big granny's kiss.

Florence and Harold had been over to Paris a couple of times to see Zella and Beverly, so Beverly knew who granny and grandpops were. Patsy simply adored Beverly as well, she would give her the biggest hugs. She couldn't wait to have children of her own. She had told Derick she wanted to start trying for a baby soon after they were married and he was more than happy to start a family

Patsy had really changed in the last five months, she had really grown up. Derick was obviously good for her. Zella could see that and was really happy for her.

Derick had wanted Alden to be his best man but he hadn't quite recovered enough for the trip, or that's what he told Derick anyway. Derick suspected it was so he didn't have to see Zella, it was his way of trying to forget her. He had no idea if it was working or not.

After the wedding Zella and Beverly went back home to Paris, accompanied by Patsy and Derick. They stayed at Zella's for their honeymoon. They wanted to do some sight-seeing so they were out more often than not. They loved the little village and all the markets and Patsy cooked a meal for her sister and her niece to say thank you for letting them spend their honeymoon there.

Chapter 37

Summer in Hampshire

Alden and Sid were sat chatting, putting the world to rights, when the nurse walked in.

"You have a visitor, Alden."

"Oh…"

At that moment, Derick popped his head round the door .

"Hi Al, Sid… "

"Hey bud… How the hell are you?"

"Well… I'm going to be a dad."

"Oh, that is great news, congratulations!"

Sid was about to leave. "You don't have go, Sid…" said Derick.

"You must have things to talk about?"

"Noooo… well, yes – but you don't have leave."

"Are you sure, lad?"

"Yeah…"

"Alden, I need to tell you something."

"What?"

"It's about Zella."

"No, no, no, I don't want to know. I've made my decision about Zella."

Derick became quite angry. "You made *your* decision, but what about *her*? Who are you to make that decision for her?"

Alden looked up at Derick a little stunned, "I told you…"

"She should just forget you."

"Go now, Derick."

"You don't deserve her!"

"Leave now and don't come back!"

"Don't worry,I'm going. She's happy in Paris, by the way."

"*Paris?*"

Derick pushed Zella's address into his hand. Alden looked down at the piece of paper, screwed it up and threw it across the room.

"You're a fucking idiot, Alden. You fought all the way to get her, now you're letting her go."

"Go… get out!"

"Truth hurt, does it? What is it? Do you think you're less of a man because you have a slight limp?"

"Get the fuck out!"

"I'm going!" Derick walked out not even looking back. Sid looked at him, shaking his head.

"Don't say a word Sid, please just don't." He walked past him.

Sid picked up the piece of paper up and folded it, when Alden was out of the room he slipped it into his wallet. Sadly a week later Sid passed away peacefully in his sleep. Alden was devastated, he had grown very fond of Sid.

At Sid's funeral the week later, Alden met his four sons who all looked just like him. Alden had a glimpse of a young handsome Sid. He told the boys that Sid had taken him under his wing when he had arrived at the convalescent home and made everything a little more bearable. Things were not going to be the same without Sid.

Epilogue

1964

As the weeks turned into months Alden was finally to be discharged from the nursing home and was on his way back to Chesterfield. When he got back home the house felt cold and lonely. It had been stood empty for months and was damp and fusty. He made the coal fire up and got it going to warm the place up.

He thought he'd better go and buy some groceries. He took a slow walk into the village, where he bought some tea, milk, bread, eggs and cheese. He knew he'd overdone it as his leg had started to throb. As he limped back he bumped in to Hilda.

"Hello Alden, how lovely to see you back."

"It's good to be back."

"That little one of your sure is a beauty."

Hilda knew Alden couldn't possibly know about his daughter and would spark some interest. Alden, for his part, thought Hilda had lost her marbles, wittering on about his little ones. She must be mixing him up with someone else, he thought. He put the thought out of his head and made his way home.

The rest of the evening, he listened to the radio and took it easy, just resting his leg. A few days later, however, someone else mentioned his little girl. He thought that maybe it was something he'd not remembered from his past, maybe all of his memory hadn't come back.

Meanwhile over in Paris

Zella was just coming back from the market in the village pushing Beverly in her pushchair as she approach the home she saw a figure at her door.

"Bonjour, vous désirez?" She shouted and the figure turned.

"Zella…"

She realised it was Michael.

"Michael… What are you doing here? How did you know I was here, more to the point?"

"Carlos gave me your address. I wanted to see you."

"Well, it's a lovely surprise."

"Carlos told me about this little beauty. I bet Alden is so proud."

"Alden doesn't know about Beverly."

"Ohhhh, I see. You never told him?"

"How could I…? He couldn't remember me. How was I going to deal with a daughter too?"

"What do you mean, he didn't remember you? He remembered you when I saw him in the hospital. He talked about you."

"When you saw him at the hospital, he remembered me? When was this?"

"When Dorian offered you the partnership

"I see…"

Zella was angry and upset all rolled into one. She assumed Alden just didn't love her and was too much of coward to tell her. Michael forgot to add a vital ingredient to the conversation: why Alden had done what he did. Perhaps this would give him a second chance with Zella.

Back in Chesterfield

Kenneth had heard that Alden was back and went round to see him. Alden was pleased to see him.

"How are you?"

"I'm good."

"Are you ready to come back to yet?"

"I'm not ready for that yet. I understand if you need to replace me."

"No, no, no, take your time. I'm glad you're alright."

"I need to sort a few things in my head before I do anything else"

"I get it. You give us such a fright."

"Yeah, I was frightened I would never walk again. That's a scary thought."

After Kenneth had left Alden felt a that sudden wave of loneliness again. The house was so quiet, the only sound was the clock tick, tick, tick, it was driving him mad. He pulled his wallet out of his pocket and, as always, there was Zella staring out at him. As he took her photo out, a piece of paper fluttered out. Alden sighed heavily because he knew what that piece of paper was and he knew who'd put it there. He gazed at Zella's beautiful face. He loved her so much, the more he stared at her the more he needed to go to her. "Thank you Sid," he whispered. Little did he know that Michael had been spending a lot of time with Zella and they had become quite close again in fact he'd asked her to marry him.

Unaware, he felt he knew what he had to do. The next morning, he headed to the estate agent and put the house up for sale. He managed to sell all his furniture, cheap for a quick sale, then he made his way to see Kenneth telling he wouldn't be coming back, he was going to Paris to be with Zella. Kenneth wished him luck and said goodbye, he was sorry to lose him and if he needed a reference he would give him one. Last but not least, he went to Derick's house. Patsy opened the door she stepped back in surprise.

"Alden…"

"Patsy, you're looking very well… and rather pregnant." He smiled.

"How are you?"

"Oh, I'm alright."

"I'm so sorry for everything. Ohhhh, Alden, please come in." And she shouted for Derick.

"Alden…Mate!" Derick was so glad to see Alden and asked him when he got back.

"A few weeks ago."

"Why didn't you come to see me? I could have picked you up…"

"I was not the nicest person the last time you saw me, I'm really sorry."

"Hey… let's forget that."

"I'm going to get her back."

"About Zella…"

"Please don't tell me she has met someone, I'm going to Paris."

"Hmmm, she's…"

"No, don't tell me anything!" He interrupted.

"When do you leave?"

"In a few weeks."

"Alden, she's getting married

"No… No…"

"She marrying Michael."

"He didn't waste any time, did he?"

"He has already booked the register office in Paris"

"Where…?"

"*Bureau de l'Etat Civil*… We're supposed to be going."

"Don't worry, Zella *will* be getting married, just not to Michael."

Patsy could see the despair in his face and how much this was hurting him and blurted out, "You have a daughter!" Alden looked at Patsy with a puzzled expression on his face, remembering what Hilda had said to him the other day.

"Daughter…?"

"Her name is Beverly."

"Derick is this true? Why didn't you tell me?"

"I tried to tell you Alden, the last day I came to see you, remember? You told me to get out."

288

Alden put his hands up to his head and through his hair. "Ohhhh…why am I such an idiot?"

"It's your natural charm!"Derick smirked.

Alden side eyed him with the hint of a laugh, shaking his head he told them he had to correct this once and for all. They asked what his plan was so he told them he would go to Paris and win her back. He had to, he couldn't live without Zella or his daughter. He wanted to get to know his little girl and Beverly needed to know who her dad was.

Derick insisted he would take him to the airport and Alden's stomach was churning, but not because of the flight. He didn't know what was going to happen. Would Zella turn him away or would she be pleased to see him?

After boarding the plane, Alden sat back in his seat trying to work out how he was going to approach Zella and explain everything. He gazed out of the window, fragments of clouds scattered about the sky. He watched the drifting mist descend on the ocean, the engines roaring as he sailed through the sky.

The plane started its descent into Charles de Gaulle airport. It came in low and there was a jolt as the wheels hit the tarmac. He checked in then, grabbed his bag and hailed a taxi. As they pulled up, Alden was puzzled.

"Hang on, this is can't be it." He said.

"Oui…"

"Are you sure…uumm, *Es-tu sûr*?"

"Oui…"

"*Ca va. Merci*."

He took the case from the boot and looked around. All he could was the factory building and he was convinced that the taxi driver had brought him to the wrong place. There was no one to ask. He walked closer then, luckily, he spotted a lady coming from the building

"Excuse me!"

The lady looked at him wondering what on earth he could want here. Maybe he wanted to make an order, she knew he was British, she could tell by his accent. By chance, Miriam and Carlos were coming from the flat. Carlos saw Alden and shouted down to him.

"Carlos, Thank God for that. I thought I was at the wrong place."

"What are you doing here, Alden?"

"I've come to get my Zella back."

"You know she's getting married right"

"So I heard."

"You can't be here, Alden"

"Why not…?"

"You hurt her badly."

Miriam intervened. She placed her hand on Carlos's arm and told him he shouldn't interfere.

She could see how much Alden loved Zella and what an awful mess it all was, but at the end of the day, if they loved each other, they should be together.

"Let him go to her, Carlos." Miriam said smiling at Alden.

She believed in love conquering all and they were meant to be together, it would work out how it was meant to be. Carlos nodded and wished him luck, because he was going to need it. He and Miriam walked slowly away, leaving Alden heading up the stair toward the door. He knocked on the door and waited a few minutes before he heard footsteps. As Zella opened the door she recognised the figure standing there and she just stood there, frozen to the spot.

"Zella…"

Zella just starred at Alden with her mouth open she couldn't believe he was actually standing there in front of her.

"Alden…?"

"Zella, I'm so sorry…"

"I'm so pleased you have got your memory back," she hurled at him sarcastically.

He moved closer, "I'm so sorry… I never meant to hurt you…

"But You Did!"

"I was stupid, to let you go like that."

Zella slapped his face hard, leaving a red handprint, "How could you do that to me?"

"I…I…" he spluttered, taken back by the violence of her reaction.

"You purposely let me think you didn't know me. It was cruel, you broke my heart in to a million pieces."

"I know… I know…"

He could see the anger in Zella's eyes and he knew there was another slap coming, his cheek couldn't take another like the one before it stung and was still burning his face. He held his hands up ready.

"Zella…please let me explain before you wallop me again."

"Leave!"

"Please don't send me away."

"I'm getting married."

Alden begged her not to do this again, it would be another mistake

"Just leave!"

"I want to see my daughter."

Zella looked stunned. How he could he know about Beverly?

"I have missed a year of my daughter life, I won't miss another day. You talk of hurt and lies but you kept my daughter from me."

"No... I didn't. You pretended not to know who I was. How was I supposed to tell you about our daughter, and then, of course, you disappeared."

Alden sighed, she was right. He did do that.

"I'm getting married, Alden."

"No... you're not."

"I beg your pardon?"

"I want to see Beverly."

Zella didn't want to stop him knowing his little girl and told him he'd better come in and there, in her playpen looking up at him was Beverly. His heart melted and a tear ran from his eye down his cheek. Turning, he told Zella she had the look of his mother. Tenderly, he picked Beverly up, kissing her cheek and stroking her strawberry blonde curls. She giggled at him. Placing her hand on his face, she gently put he lips to his and softly kissed her daddy. Zella thought it was the most beautiful thing she had ever seen.

"Please don't take her away from me."

"I would never do that."

"I did what I did for a reason, didn't Michael tell you?"

"What reason…?" she asked.

"I didn't want to get in the way of your career, you'd just been offered the partnership… you were on your way to becoming a famous designer – I couldn't take that away from you."

Zella couldn't believe Michael had missed that bit out, was it accidental or deliberate? Again her life had been turned upside down and she had some thinking to do. Alden *was* the love of her life, that was never going to change.

The next day she was sat with Miriam chatting over lunch

"How are you, Zella dear?"

"You mean after seeing Alden?

"Yes…"

"I don't know what to do."

"If your heart is telling you that Alden is the one then you *can't* marry Michael. Remember what happened with Clive."

"Ohhhh Miriam, why is my life so complicated?"

Miriam let Zella into a little secret. She had met Carlos in Greece when he was still married to his first wife. She'd fallen head over heels and they made love under the stars. Carlos was supposed to leave his wife and be with her but he never did so she married someone else, someone she didn't love. It was many years later she met Carlos again, when they were both divorced.

"It was like we had never been apart."

"How romantic." Zella oozed.

"He asked me to marry him right there on the spot."

"Oooo, I didn't realise Carlos was so romantic."

"We were married and we have never looked back. So, my love, really think about what your next move is going to be."

A few days later, Patsy and Derick flew over with new daughter Tina, for the wedding. They were staying with Zella, as were their mother and Harold who were looking forward to spending some quality time with both their granddaughters. Zella was making a special meal for them all, she'd also invited Carlos and Miriam, but before that she told Michael about Alden's visit. Michael knew in his heart things were about to go horribly wrong.

"What did Alden tell you in the hospital?"

"What do you mean?"

"Michael, I think you know exactly what I mean…"

"No…"

"You're lying!"

"Zella, he *remembered* you."

"Yes, he told me. Did you know why he pretended not to know me?"

"No…"

"Michael?"

"OK, yes… I had an idea"

At that moment everyone had started to arrive.

Carlos felt the tension and suggested that they all went out

"We'll all go out for dinner and leave you two to it."

"It's fine, Carlos, honestly."

"My darling, I think you two need to talk."

He swiftly gathered Miriam, Patsy Derick Florence and Harold and the two babies and shooed them out of the apartment, leaving Zella and Michael alone.

At a little bistro about a mile or so away, Carlos and Miriam entertained their guests.

"She won't marry Michael!" Pasty blurted out .

Florence wanted to know why, and if this had something to do with Alden. Patsy told her it had *everything* to do with Alden, and she would never feel the same way about any other man. Miriam agreed with Patsy and Florence knew Patsy was right.

At that moment, Alden walked in and saw Derick and everyone. Florence got up from the table and slapped him across the face.

"How dare you hurt my daughter!"

"Wow, what is it with everyone wanting to hit me? I love your daughter." He picked Beverly up from the high chair. "I deserved that slap but you must know Zella is everything to me and so is this little girl. I'm going to make everything alright."

"You better!"

❧ ❧

Back at the flat

"Promise, Michael, you didn't leave that out on purpose?"

"I promise."

Michael looked down at his feet. "I do love you."

Zella felt it had been one big mess from start to finish. It all had to stop right here, right now. She was going to marry Michael. She did, however, tell him that Alden would always be Beverly's father and he would always be in her life. Michael told her he understood but he wanted children of his own as well.

When the family came back, they put the children to bed and they all sat round the log fire discussing the wedding. Patsy wondered what the hell Zella was doing. She knew Alden was always going to be the one she loved, so why was she going ahead with the wedding?

"Anyone fancy some hot chocolate?" She asked.

Every one said yes, which was what Patsy had hoped. She wanted to get Zella alone in the kitchen.

"Zella, can you help me please?"

"Yes, of course."

Patsy put a pan of milk on the stove.

"What are you *doing*?"

"Helping you with the chocolate…"

"No, Zella, I mean with this wedding!"

"Hmmm… getting married."

"Do you love Michael…? I don't think you do. I'll tell you what you're doing, you're running away again!" Patsy said forcefully.

Zella looked at Patsy a little puzzled. She *did* love Michael, but was it the right kind of love, the love that you want to spend your life with? Or was it like you love your *friend*?

Now Patsy had put the question into Zella's mind and she wasn't quite as sure as she thought she had been. She had married Clive and that hadn't worked out because of the way she felt about Alden, was she about to do the same again? It wasn't just herself Zella had to thing about, now she had Beverly too. Things hadn't exactly gone smoothly and a lot had happened. She was worried that things would go wrong as they had in the past. She clung to the fact that Michael loved her and Beverly.

"I don't want to talk about this."

"No... because you don't want to face your feelings. You love one man and one man only and *you know it!*"

"Enough, Patsy. I don't want to talk about this anymore... EVER!!! I plan to marry Michael tomorrow." She quickly took the tray and went back to the others.

Patsy wasn't going to let Zella make another mistake. Even though she liked Michael she knew it was a mistake. She had finally grown up and she knew this entire mess was down to her..

The next morning Patsy asked Derick where Alden was staying.

"We are going to go and see him."

He wanted to know why, so she explained what she was planning.

"You are interfering."

"My sister should be happy... and Alden is *the one.*"

Patsy thought that by intervening she could make everything she had done in the past all right again.

The morning of the wedding

Zella was busy getting Beverly ready. She had made her the prettiest dresses for her and Tina, Beverly toddled out to Florence, with Harold close behind her. She was a little beauty, little blonde ringlets framing her little face making her big blue eyes stand out. Derick followed with Tina in his arms, equally as pretty. Florence was so proud of her little granddaughters and she and Harold played with the children whilst Zella and Patsy got ready.

Zella had bought a beautiful, dusky pink dress with a cut out detail dropping to a line of buttons, finishing the look with an elegant headband. When she stepped out from the bedroom, Harold was overwhelmed.

"Oh my, Zella, it will be an honour walking beside you at the register office."

"Thank you... Dad."

Zella had just made Harold's day. He felt so proud, he had never been a dad.

They all made their way in to town to the Bureau d'Etat, where Michael was waiting. Patsy looked around anxiously.

"Come on, come on..." she murmured under her breath.

They were all just about to go in to the registrar when Alden strode up and shouted for Zella who turned.

"Please don't..."

"Go away, Alden...." Michael shouted angrily.

"No... I'm not leaving without Zella or my daughter."

Michael angrily pushed Alden,. Still a little unsteady on his feet, Alden stumbled backwards, losing his footing and falling to the floor. Zella screamed than to help Alden while Derick stepped in front of Michael telling him to back off. In the confusion, Beverly let go of Miriam's hand and toddled up to Zella, wrapped her arms round her and kissed Alden gently on the cheek.

"Are you alright?" Zella asked, helping Alden back to his feet.

"Yeah..." He picked Beverly up.

"You're spoiling my wedding day. Leave, Alden."
 Michael shouted.

"I told you – I'm not leaving without Zella and Beverly."

"You are getting on my nerves now, Alden. Leave or I
  will have you thrown out."

Thing were getting heated and Zella asked her mother and
Miriam to take the children outside. Miriam tried to take
Beverly from Alden, but she didn't want to leave him and
began to cry. Alden soothed her and said he would come
back to her in a little while.

"Zella, can we get on with our wedding day now?"

Zella looked at Michael then looked at Alden.

"Zella…?"

Michael knew she wasn't going to go through with their
wedding, he could see it in her eyes. She had turned to
Patsy, who was shaking her head, mouthing, *'Don't do it!'*

"Zella, please don't do this." Alden pleaded.

She stared at Alden then turned her head to look straight at
Michael

"I'm sorry, Michael."

Alden sighed deeply with relief.

"Zella…?"

"I can't, Michael…"

Michael closed his eyes and sighed, lowering his head.

"I'm so sorry"

"So am I…"

Michael had rushed out so quickly that Florence, Harold,
Miriam and Carlos knew that the wedding wasn't taking

place. When Patsy and Derick came out they confirmed it. They all settled to wait outside for Zella and Alden.

Alden moved towards Zella, "I'm sorry, but I just couldn't let you go."

"I know…"

"I love you."

"I love you too and it's quite clear that Beverly loves you, the way she wanted to comfort you."

"She knows I'm her daddy."

"I think you're right."

Alden kissed her and suggested that they take their little girl home. They made their way out to the others and went back to the flat where Florence and Miriam had prepared a wedding lunch. Alden took Florence and Harold to one side and apologised.

"It's always been you, Alden. Don't you ever let her down again."

"I don't intend to ever let her or Beverly out of my life again"

Florence went over to Zella and hugged her, "I love you, Zella. All I want is for you and Beverly to be happy… Are you truly happy Zella?"

"Yes… I love him, Mum."

Florence smiled and nodded her head, "I know…"

Zella watched Alden with Beverly. He was so good with her, she could hear Beverly laughing as Alden made silly faces at her. Her eyes begin to fill up.

"I should be so angry with you," she said gently caressing his face.

He nodded in agreement and, taking her hand, he asked if he could feed Beverly and put her to bed, he had a bit of catching up to do.

Derick and Patsy were taking Alden's hotel room so Alden, Zella and Beverly could spend the evening alone together. As everyone called it a night and headed off, Zella wondered what had happened to Alden, it seemed like he had been gone hours. She thought maybe Beverly was playing up for him, but when she peeped around the door Alden was just sat there, watching her sleep.

"Alden?" She whispered.

Alden turned to Zella and smiled, "She's just so perfect."

Zella smiled, "Yes, she is."

"I just can't believe she's come from me, she's so beautiful."

"She takes after her mother," Zella giggled.

Alden got up and took Zella by the hand, leading her to the hall. "She is just like you. I'm so sorry I've been such a fool."

"Come on…"

He took hold of her, kissing her tenderly. She responded lovingly taking hold of his hand and leading him to the bedroom. He gently pushed his finger through her hair, his lips warm and urgent yet demanding. They undressed each other slowly. Laying still, he caressed her cheek, just like he had that first night in his car all those years ago. It was like they had never been apart, Slowly he gave her butterfly kisses down her down her neck and shoulders, all the way to the gentle swell of her breasts. Her skin tingled as his lips moved further down her body. Finally, he took her hands and clasping them tightly pushed himself between her thighs, pressing down on her, letting her feel how hard his manhood was. Then he was inside her, thrusting harder and deeper until, suddenly, her body stiffened as she climaxed. He came seconds later, flopping in a heap next to her. Smiling, he turned over, playing with a strand of hair that had fallen across her face. He blurted out, *"Marry me…"*

Zella looked deep into his eyes and told him 'yes'. "After every thing they had been through, she wasn't about to lose him again.

❧ ❧

Six months later, Zella and Alden were married. Zella had bought a dress by Fiona Hobbs, a new upcoming designer. She had seen some of her designs being made up in the factory and had met up with her when she came over to pick them up. Zella and Fiona became good friends and she asked Fiona if she would consider designing her wedding dress for her. For her part, Fiona was thrilled at the idea of making Zella Russell's wedding dress.

It was the most elegant wedding dress, sophisticated but flirtatious. With an alluring off the shoulder soft cowl neckline, front and back, with a delicate shoestring tie across back, shoulders simple but yet beautiful. The whole falling to the floor, sweeping behind with a trim of frills.

Together with their family, Derick and a heavily pregnant Patsy, Florence and Harold, Carlos and Miriam, they had the most wonderful wedding day.

Printed in Great Britain
by Amazon